Willhelm Shakespear

Songs, poems and sonnets

Edited with a critical introd

Willhelm Shakespear

Songs, poems and sonnets
Edited with a critical introd

ISBN/EAN: 9783337175955

Printed in Europe, USA, Canada, Australia, Japan

Cover: Foto ©Andreas Hilbeck / pixelio.de

More available books at **www.hansebooks.com**

THE
SONGS, POEMS, AND SONNETS

OF

WILLIAM SHAKESPEARE.

Edited, with a Critical Introduction,

BY WILLIAM SHARP.

"Shine forth, thou Starre of Poets."
—BEN JONSON.

LONDON:

Walter Scott, 24 Warwick Lane, Paternoster Row,

AND NEWCASTLE-ON-TYNE.

1885.

INDEX

TO CONTENTS AND FIRST LINES.

THE SONGS.

THE SONNETS.

POEMS.

NOTES.

from their inner consciousness strange and monstrous imaginings have restricted themselves to solving, or endeavouring to solve, certain points of strictly personal or merely clerical dubiety. Preeminently is the gratitude of students—that is of all lovers of Shakespeare's poetic work—due to that accomplished writer and Shakespearian authority, Professor Dowden ; to the late J. P. Collier ; to Mr. Thomas Tyler ; to Mr. Furnival ; to Messrs. Clarke and Wright, the Cambridge editors ; to Mr. Palgrave ; to Professor W. Minto ; to Mr. W. M. Rosetti ; to Mr. Theodore Watts ; to Mr. David Main ; to Mr. Hall Caine ; and, among foreign writers, M. Taine in France, to Mr. Grant White and Miss Hillard in America. No one of these eminent students (or of others whose names I do not at the moment recall) has permitted his or her mental vision to be obscured by the bewildering conjectural mists arising out of that miasma of sheer foolishness along whose illusive banks have strayed so many witless wanderers. They one and all see in the first series of Sonnets (i. to xcvi.) nothing but a plain declaration of the writer's loyal, self-renouncing, nobly persistent love for a younger and perhaps not wholly worthy friend ; and with but one exception* they recognize in the remainder,

* Professor Minto,—who regards the Woman-Series not in the light of a personal revelation, but as "exercises of skill undertaken in a spirit of wanton defiance and derision of commonplace"—a view first enunciated by Mr. Henry Brown, who particularized Michael Drayton and John Davies as the writers who were specially though indirectly thus satirised.

the 'Dark Woman' series (cxxvii. to clii.), the revelation of a great passion that for a season rendered full of bitter import the life of the greatest of our countrymen.

Among the most eminent poets of our own time, only Mr. Robert Browning has doubted Skakespeare's having shown us glimpses of his direct personal experience. We all know Wordsworth's famous words in his sonnet on 'The Sonnet,' *with this same key Shakespeare unlocked his heart:* to this Mr. Browning takes objection, adding "Did Shakespeare? If so, the less Shakespeare he!"—a metrical criticism that brought forth the counter-remark of Mr. Swinburne, 'No whit the less like Shakespeare, but undoubtedly the less like Browning.' Shelley, Keats, Coleridge, and Wordsworth indubitably held the personal theory, as, later, have Mr. Swinburne, the late Dante Gabriel Rosetti, Victor Hugo, and others, whose opinions, by virtue of their own poetic powers, may be considered worthy of special attention.

It may well be asked, Why should there be this persistent digging for hidden significance in the work of a man whose genius was no more secretive than that of any other dramatist? We do not speculate wildly on all possible meanings that human ingenuity is capable of twisting out of the *Amoretti* of Spenser or the *Astrophel and Stella* of Sir Philip Sydney: why then should we approach Shakespeare's sonnets as if they were the profoundest enigmas?

One reason undoubtedly lies in the senseless habit of insincere laudation that prevails to such extent. Out of every twenty who speak of Shakespeare as the greatest intellect since Æschylus and Plato, are there ten who have ever read all his writings? Are there five who intimately know them? Are there even two who find endless pleasure, wonder, suggestion, comfort, inspiration, in the sonnets? It is to be feared not : it is to be feared that there are too many whose loud appreciation of Shakespeare's greatness is based merely on an acquaintance with Mr. Irving in the characters of Hamlet and Shylock—with Miss Terry in those of Portia and Ophelia. There is perhaps no greater test of Shakespeare's overwhelming genius than the circumstance that it successfully withstands the rank incense with which it is assailed by fools and all manner of thoughtless persons, a cloud of indiscriminate praise sufficient to obscure all but the loftiest summits in the serene region of the intellect. And it is this universal *Ave! Imperator Poetarum* that is at least in part responsible for the innumerable vagaries of psychological commentators, this, coupled with an inherent preference on their part for darkness rather than for light. Realising that the greatest creator of multiform types of humanity is held in such universal esteem, they seem to consider it incumbent upon them to prove that he was not a man like as we are ; that in all things he was perfect, a flawless man, more ideal than any one of his most ideal conceptions.

What folly is this ? Granting for a moment that Shakespeare could have been the divine being some of his admirers would fain make him out, where could he have gained those experiences that render his imaginative work quick with vitality ; where could he have laid in that ballast of practical knowledge without which the ship of his genius would have sailed across no turbulent ocean of human life, traversed no perilous shoals of danger and death, but have been borne irresistibly away by any casual wind to speedy wreckage on the rocks of reality, or have foundered helplessly as soon as the transient sunshine had given place to darkness and storm ? Whatever else he was, we may rest assured that he was pre-eminently manly, and therefore that he experienced all those emotions to which men are ordinarily liable ; that he wrestled with temptations even as we ourselves do ; that not infrequently, especially in the impulsive ardours of youth, indiscretion overcame precept and prudence ; that occasionally he spoke and acted as he would fain not have done ; that once or twice, at least, in his life he had bitter cause to bewail the domination of the body, the surrender of the better part of him.* The magnetism of all genuine work of Shakespeare lies in its essential humanity : no one lives but could find his most salient mental and spiritual traits delineated somewhere in that marvellous gallery of portraits comprised in *The Plays.* Could this man, who touched to such keen music all the notes of humanity, who sounded the subtlest spiritual chords, who produced the saddest as well as the most joyous, the most majestic strains along the whole diapason of life and death, could this man have been otherwise than a veritable fellow

* *Vide*, in further confirmation, the remarkable sonnet, No. cxix.

r must the fact be overlooked that at anyrate
nportant section of these revelations—to us so
/ interesting—was never published by him
directly or indirectly, so far as has been
ained. He was not the kind of man to invite
orld in general to share in his private hopes
ars, his trials of friendship, his love-agonies.
" W. H." series, or probably but a limited
r thereof, circulated among a few friends and
cquaintances, possibly not at Shakespeare's
e at all (possibly, even, with only his half-
consent), but at that of young Herbert, or
that of some friend of the latter and generous
r of the former. That the young poet did
k upon the authorship of the sonnets as dis-
e is evident from these lines in sonnet lxxvi :

Thy write I still all one, even the same,
nd keep invention in a noted weed,
     (*i.e., in a known, a recognisable style.*)
iat every word doth almost tell my name,
owing their birth and where they did proceed?"

at he intended their ultimate publication in
erally accepted sense of the word may with
e certainty be inferred from internal evidence:
last lines of Sonnet xxxviii :—

my slight Muse do please these curious days,
e pain be mine, but thine shall be the praise."

was not till many years after their composi-
verse in date as they are) that they were
d in book form, and even then they had not
thor's supervision, if even his direct consent
· collective issue. It is certainly unlikely

that he would have published the *two series* as t
appear in the Quarto of 1609, Nos. cxxvii. to
being beyond doubt antecedent in compositior
those, or to the great majority of those, addres
to " W. H."

In the very evident deficiency in strict sequei
and in the equally manifest want of arrangem
according to persons and periods, is alone aln:
sufficient basis for the argument that Shakespe
wrote these sonnets *not* as literary exercises but
genuine expressions of emotion, either when {
swayed by this emotion, or when stirred by vi
remembrance. One or two of the sonnets, pe
liarly suited for adaptation, he interpolated
one of his early comedies, *Love's Labour's L*
Otherwise, it is generally understood that the f
printed sonnets of Shakespeare are those surr
titiously given by Jaggard in his quaintly-sty
miscellany, *The Passionate Pilgrim* (published
1599).   How Jaggard obtained these and otl
pieces we do not know, though it is of cou
possible that he applied to one who was alrea
heralded as a coming luminary, a master of me
fluous verse,* and obtained permission to pr
them, the young poet all the while not suspecti
that the authorship of the whole miscellany was
be attributed to him.   But against this suppositi
there are serious objections.   Firstly (but this is

---

* Francis Meres in his *Palladis Tamia, Wit's Treasi*
(published in 1598), speaks of the "sweete wittie soule
Ovid" living "in mellifluous and honey-tongued Shak
peare," and refers, *inter alia*, to his " sugred sonnets amo
his private friends."

ninor importance) the two opening sonnets differ considerably in details from their counterparts (Nos. cxxxvii. and cxliv.) in Thomas Thorpe's edition of the Complete Sonnets, published ten years later. This might either point to the fact that Shakespeare altered the misreadings, or improved the original versions, in his own $\frac{or}{and}$ other copies of *The Passionate Pilgrim*—corrections which duly came under the notice of Thorpe : or else it might point to Jaggard having taken them down on hearsay, or having copied them from unrevised or carelessly replicated versions. Secondly, it is not likely that Shakespeare would have given any compiler mere studies, as undoubtedly are the 'Venus and Adonis' sonnets and Divisions Nos. iv., vi., ix., and xi. of *The Passionate Pilgrim*, especially in incomplete form (as is Div. ix., which wants the second line) : charming as they are, though too characteristic of an age differing essentially from our own to be suited for 'a mixed audience,' they are manifestly but studies for, or contemporary offshoots from, the composition of *Venus and Adonis*, published from five to six years before the appearance of Jaggard's miscellany. Thirdly, still less would he be likely to contribute odd stanzas, as Divisions x. and xiii. (probably draft-portions of, or excerpts from, an unpublished elegiac poem —printed in this volume under the title *Death in Youth* and *Beauty*), or Divisions xiv. and xv., disconnected sets, probably part of a contemplated, an unfinished, or a lost love-poem, if indeed by Shakespeare at all.

It is, of course, somewhat puzzling to understand how such sonnets as the first three of *The Passionate Pilgrim* (in publication ten years anterior to that of the first collective edition) could have come within Jaggard's cognizance unless given him by their author. It is almost certain that they were portions of the series addressed to the woman who was at one time Shakespeare's mistress, and if so, is it likely, records of strong emotion and bitter experience as they are, that he would have handed them over to an adventurous publisher? It would be easy, of course, to make one surmise after another in favour of the young poet's having done so, but where there is little light to go by, we must follow what seems most like a gleam of dayshine, and not every illusive will-o-the-wisp that flickers along the difficult way. For my part, I can only surmise that (1) Shakespeare showed these and other love-sonnets to his friend Herbert before the latter became his rival, or else subsequently to the desertion of the latter in turn (or *his* of the Dark Woman), and that Herbert (or Earl of Pembroke as, in the event of the latter supposition being correct, he would be) showed them to a friend or friends, through whom they reached Jaggard : *or* (2) that Shakespeare's mistress herself, in a spirit of wanton indifference, mockery, or jealousy (hoping to stir up a real dissension between the two friends who loved her) showed or gave them to Pembroke, or perhaps out of sheer vanity allowed them to be copied by more or less disinterested acquaintances : *or* (3)—and this seems to me the likeliest of all— the whole body of the sonnets was never actually sent to his mistress at all, but in the main simply constituted Shakespeare's contemporary record of the passion that so deeply affected his life at that period. This record he may at a later period have shown to Pembroke or some other friend, and so indirectly brought about their ultimate publication. Individual sonnets, as those of "The Passionate Pilgrim," *not necessarily revealing the genuine standpoint of the writer*, may have been previously permitted to circulate in manuscript. What lover would ever have written to his mistress sonnets—*i.e.*, missives intended for her receipt—containing such remarks as

> "*For I have sworn thee fair, and thought thee bright,*
> *Who art as black as hell, as dark as night!*"
>
> (S. 147.)

or

> "*For I have sworn thee fair; more perjured I*
> *To swear against the truth so foul a lie.*"
>
> (S. 152.)

Probably, out of the twenty-six, eleven (Ss. 128, 131 to 136 inclusive, 139, 140, 143, and 149) were actually sent to his mistress at different periods : the remainder (even including a sonnet like cl., with its 'thou's') I conjecture to have been—as already stated—pages of what may be called Shakespeare's private journal of his passion, and certainly not love-missives. Not improbably they form as they stand a genuine sequence, their author having either sent copies of certain of them after their entry in his MS. book, or, as is more likely, made the entries in the latter from originals duly sent.

Nos. cxxix., cxliv., cxlvi., are surely not such missives as he would have sent to the woman he loved or had loved : such a procedure would be contrary both to his own chivalrous nature and the spirit of the times. Cxli. itself affords fairly conclusive proof that at any rate *all* the sonnets were not sent : for in addition to its being such a missive as no lover, in whatever mood, would send to his *inamorata,* it may be noted that the personal address characterizing the opening lines is forgotten in the couplet, where ' she ' usurps ' thou.'

The chief points of difficulty, and of critical dissensions, are, broadly speaking, five in number : *viz.* (1) The sphinx-like Dedication ; (2) The identity of the friend of sonnets i. to cxxvi. ; (3) The identity of the Rival Poet referred to in this series ; (4) The arrangement of the sonnets in groups ; and (5) The identity of the inspirer of sonnets cxxvii. to clii., and the connection of the latter, if any, with the preceding series.

As briefly as possible these points must now be considered. It is possible that in endeavouring to be succinct, the editor may appear not only to take too much as indisputable, but also to assert what he has to say with an air of dogmatism : if either failing be apparent, the fault should be attributed not to him who sins unintentionally, but to the mass of commentary he has waded through, in the atmosphere involving which he has for some time past been saturated. To one who looks at the moot points with unprejudiced eyes, and with some necessary knowledge of the social manners as well as of the literature of the period in question, so much of what has been written on the subject seems such mere superfluity of foolishness that he almost inevitably comes to regard points of manifest likeli-hood as points of irrefutable certainty. Again, there is not room in a mere prefatory note, such as this, to go into ample detail in support of assever-ations : students will find what they want in the writings of Professor Dowden and other ac-complished Shakespearian scholars, while ordinary readers must be content to accept in faith what is undoubtedly representative of the most recent Shakespearian criticism. For this I am indebted to Professor Dowden, Mr. Thomas Tyler, Professor Minto, and others, who directly or indirectly have afforded me valuable data to work upon. Especially in connection with Part II. of the sonnets have I to acknowledge my indebtedness to the careful research and critical acumen displayed in Mr. Tyler's introduction to the shortly to be published pho.o-lithographic facsimile of the sonnets as they appear in the first Quarto (1609).*

(1.) *The Dedication.* The opening words have themselves been productive of some misunder-standing. *The onlie begetter :* not unnaturally the word 'only' has been taken by many, unacquainted with the change in significance which so many of our words have undergone, to mean *sole.* Its real meaning in the phrase quoted may possibly, how-ever, be 'matchless' or 'incomparable' or 'super-excellent,' or some other such superlative. When

* Photographed from the copy in the British Museum, and published by Mr. C. Praetorius, 14 Clareville Grove, Hereford Square, S.W.

in Sonnet i. Shakespeare speaks of "*the only herald of the gaudy Spring*" he does not mean 'sole herald' but 'most welcome' or 'incomparable,' or perhaps 'chief.' *Begetter :* still more is misunderstanding liable to be caused by this word. It has been taken to signify the person who procured the sonnets for the publisher Thorpe, 'the only procurer, collector, begetter' (here 'only' signifying 'sole'). As Professor Tyler has pointed out, there is just a possibility that Thorpe meant to convey to their problematical 'procurer' the assurance that the poet's promise of 'eternitie' would be literally fulfilled unto him for the great service he had rendered to literature in obtaining these sonnets for publication. But neither Mr. Tyler nor any of the most eminent recent commentators entertain these suppositions. The word *begetter* is now understood to have signified *originator, source of, cause of.* When in Sonnet xxxviii. Shakespeare addresses his friend, "*Be thou the tenth Muse . . . and he that calls on thee, let him bring forth Eternal numbers to outlive long date,*" the reference is undoubtedly the same as that underlying 'begetter.' "The onlie begetter" therefore may either be "the sole bringer forth, the sole cause of," or else "the incomparable inspirer" of 'these insuing sonnets.'

(2.) *The Identity of "Mr. W. H."* Even a superficial reader would—notwithstanding a few puzzling expressions—speedily gather that Sonnets i. to cxxvi. were addressed to a dearly loved male friend of the writer : probably, also, that they constituted a more or less discernible sequence. Of long continuance, and characterized by a great amount of argumentative energy, has been the debate concerning the identity of this friend, obscurely shrouded under those puzzling initials which Mr. Thomas Thorpe so little thought were doomed to be the cause of such an amount of perplexed discussion.

The researches of critical students ultimately made it plain that the Dedicatee must have been one of two men, Henry Wriothesley, Earl of Southampton, and William Herbert, Earl of Pembroke. It might seem easy to at once fix upon the latter as the " W. H." of Mr. Thorpe, but the fact of these initials corresponding with those of Pembroke is by no means sufficient for identification. I shall not attempt in the limited space at my command to repeat all the *pros* and *cons* on either side, but may at once state that though many influential commentators have considered Southampton to be the individual referred to, it is now known, almost certainly beyond disproof, that Shakespeare's friend was William Herbert, Earl of Pembroke. For the claims of Lord Southampton it may briefly be said that it was to this nobleman (who was not more than nine years the junior of the poet) that Shakespeare in 1593 dedicated his *Venus and Adonis*, and in the following year his *Rape of Lucrece*, on this second occasion using dedicatory words of such warmth of expression as nearly to coincide with the ardent language of some of the most directly personal of the sonnets. Especially is Sonnet xxvi. considered more like the method of address which Shakespeare would have pursued in the case of Lord Southampton, than of the much younger and distinctly less staid Earl of Pembroke. Again, Shakespeare in this preface says plainly to his older friend " what I have done is yours ; what I have to do is yours." As for the fact that the initials in Thorpe's dedication are ' W. H.' and not ' H. W.,' it has been contended that the transposition was intentional and was meant as a blind—a rather far fetched conclusion certainly, considering all the circumstances. As for the ' Mr.,' no blind, in all probability, was thereby meant. The prefix at that period had a much more elastic use than now ; examples of its similar employment could easily be adduced—*e.g.*, in *England's Parnassus* Lord Buckhurst appears as *M.* Sackville.

But an overwhelming amount of evidence—facts of minor weight mostly, but all tending in the same direction—renders it as nearly indisputable as any question can be without *absolutely* conclusive evidence, that the ' W. H.' of the sonnets was the Earl of Pembroke. Any remaining doubts in the minds of those who have perused the lucid arguments of Professor Minto in 'Characteristics of English Poets' (section on *The Elizabethan Sonneteers*), of Professor Dowden, and others, must be removed after acquaintance with the latest researches as set forth by Mr. Thomas Tyler in his Introduction to Mr. Praetorius' Quarto-Facsimile. Here we clearly learn all that is necessary concerning Pembroke's life,—his friendship with Shakespeare, his *liaison* with the same woman who at one time was the latter's mistress (certainly in the poetic, and only less certainly in the more commonly accepted meaning of the term)—that mysterious 'Dark Woman,' now for the first time, in all probability, identified—his Court troubles, his public career. Sixteen years younger than the great dramatist, brilliant in varied accomplishments and in manners, beautiful and well worthy of the famous race with whom he was so closely connected, it was this William Herbert, Earl of Pembroke, to whom as 'the real source of the insuing sonnets' Thomas Thorpe, with or without the knowledge or consent of the popular nobleman $\frac{and}{or}$ his already famous friend, inscribed his celebrated dedication. The Dedication, therefore, may be taken to read thus : *To the Sole Cause (or Incomparable Inspirer) of these insuing sonnets—Mr. W[illiam] H[erbert] (Earl of Pembroke)—all Happiness, and that Eternity promised by our immortal poet, their author, wisheth the well-wishing 'adventurer' in issuing them in printed form, T[homas] T[horpe].*

(3) To Professor Minto is due the discovery of the Rival Poet specially referred to by Shakespeare in one of the nine sonnets (lxxviii.-lxxxvi.) dealing with the pretentions of other bardic aspirants for the favour of his patron-friend. Almost every likely writer had been cited as the 'better spirit' of sonnet lxxx., the 'proud full sail of whose great verse' threatened to altogether obliterate from notice his own 'saucy bark.' Marlowe, notwithstanding certain indubitable drawbacks to the likelihood of the supposition, and Ben Jonson, were the two generally considered as having claims to be nominated this rival poet. " I hope," says Professor

Minto, " I shall not be held guilty of hunting after paradox if I say that every possible poet has been named but the right one, nor of presumption if I say that he is so obvious that his escape from notice is something little short of miraculous." With conclusive argument Mr. Minto then proceeds to prove that Chapman was this poet, a conclusion now accepted by all students as definite.

(4.) *The arrangement of the Sonnets in groups.* It may be broadly taken for granted that any transposition of certain groups of the sonnets should not be attempted. They may, as they stand, be productive of no inconsiderable perplexity, but if every commentator had his way the confusion would in a very short time become hopeless. The example of Mr. Gerald Massey may be held forth as a solemn warning : to the meditative student none could be more salutary.

The only certain division is that of sonnets cxxvii. to clii. from the 126 preceding : as yet, perhaps, the only defensible transposition would be the placement of cxxvii.-clii. before and not after the longer series, belonging as they do to an earlier period, not only in application, but as regards composition : moreover, this transposition would render certain portions in the subsequent series less obscure, and would indeed throw a flood of light thereupon which every one who read the sonnets for the first time would find sufficiently illuminative. Merely as a matter of personal opinion the present editor would like to see the ' Dark Woman ' series placed—as an interlude— between sonnets xxxix. and xl. Here the series would fit in with peculiar applicability. In one or two of the immediately preceding sonnets (especially xxxv.) there are foreshadowings of what is taking, or has taken place : then would come the long passion-poem, revealing everything to the sympathetic reader : and, hereafter, the reproachful, forgiving, warning, consoling, beseeching series from xl. to xciv., concluding with the sonnets of Reconciliation c. to cxxvi. Certainly if I had ventured to interfere with the universally accepted numerical sequence, this is the order which I would have adopted.

The following divisional arrangement of the series addressed to 'W. H.,' is to some extent based on that of Mr. Armitage Brown, on that of Dr. Furnival in the *Leopold Shakespeare*, and on that of Mr. Tyler in his Introduction ; as for the headings of the groups, these may be altered by any reader where found unsatisfactory.

i-xvii.	Of Persuasion (to his friend 'W. H.' to marry and perpetuate his beauty and race).
xviii-xxxiii.	Of Shakespeare's ardent friendship for 'W. H.'
xxxiii-xxxix.	Of Renunciation.
xl-lviii.	Of Excuse. Love in Absence, Promised Immortality of Fame, and Remonstrance.
lix-lx.	Of Oblivion.
lxi-lxv.	Of Suffering through Love, and of Apprehension.
lxvi.	Of Deep Weariness.
lxvii-lxviii.	Of Contemplative Regret.
lxix-lxx.	Of Evil Rumours concerning 'W. H.'
lxxi-lxxiv.	Of Inevitable Death and Enduring Love.

(5.) *The Identity of the Inspirer of* cxxvii.-clii.
—The identity of the woman who for a season
exercised so potent a spell on Shakespeare has for
long remained a complete mystery ; while not
beyond conjecture, discovery seemed as hopeless
as ascertainment of ' what song the syrens sang.'
Even so recent and so accomplished an authority
as Professor Dowden has written, "We shall never
discover the name of the woman who for a season
could sound, as no one else, the instrument of
Shakespeare's heart from the lowest note to the
top of the compass.   To the eyes of no diver among
the wrecks of time will that curious talisman gleam."
But that curious talisman has been revealed to the
vision of Mr. Tyler ; he, and the Rev. W. A.
Harrison, and, indirectly, the late Rev. F. C. Fitton,
have solved an apparently inscrutable enigma.   I
cannot here repeat or even give a digest of all he
has to say on this interesting subject, and it must
suffice to affirm that it is now established, probably
beyond disproof, that the woman who was the
mistress first of Shakespeare and then of the Earl

of Pembroke, was known as Mrs. Mary Fitton. Mary Fitton, or Ffitton, of good parentage, was born in 1578, so that she would be about seventeen when Shakespeare first saw her, or between eighteen and nineteen when the *liaison* may have occurred (possibly it was considerably later), a conjecture founded on the fact that *Love's Labour's Lost* (containing allusive sonnets) was played at the Christmas of 1597. Whether she favoured Shakespeare while still unmarried is uncertain ; the strong probability is that it was while she was simply Mary Fitton. This fascinating woman was one of Queen Elizabeth's maids-of-honour. Her first husband was a Captain Lougher, though it was possibly before this that she scandalised the Court by being proved with child by the young Earl of Pembroke, who, while confessing the fact, utterly renounced all marriage. Mr. Tyler suggests the possibility that she had been married in very early youth, a *mariage de convenance*, in support of the existence of which he adduces strong evidence. If so, she must have secured a divorce on the legal point noted by Mr. Tyler, otherwise Pembroke would have had no need to declare his resolution not to marry Mary Fitton. The date of this scandal was 1601, a circumstance which tends to prove that the woman-sonnets were written at varying periods, and that Pembroke found passion a stronger force than the loyalty of friendship. The case would seem to be that Sir Edward Fitton, while in Ireland on political duty, arranged for his young daughter's marriage with a Captain Lougher ; that this marriage was solemnized, but afterwards annulled on account of some irregularity in money matters ; that while in London, after her father's return, Mary Fitton (having renounced the name of Lougher) saw Shakespeare acting, or otherwise made his acquaintance ; entertained a fancy and possibly a passion for him ; later on allowed Pembroke to take Shakespeare's place, and became mother of a child by the former ; got into disgrace with the Queen ; transferred her favours to Sir Richard Leveson, knight, by whom she had two illegitimate children ; and finally married her second husband, a Captain (or Mr.) Polwhele.

These circumstances are in themselves sufficient to prove that Mary Fitton was if not a woman of rare beauty at any rate one of extraordinary fascination. We know (cxxviii.) that she was a skilled musician on the virginal, surely a certain way to touch the heart of Shakespeare, the poet who of all others has written with most emphasis and unmistakable sincerity of music : that she had lovely eyes, dark and with that pathos generally accompanying depth—

> " And truly not the morning sun of heaven
> Better becomes the grey cheeks of the east,
> Nor that full star that ushers in the even
> Doth half that glory to the sober west,
> As those two mourning eyes become thy face "—

and that her mouth was formed for sweet speech and lover's kisses,

> " Those lips that Love's own hand did make."

The bitter emphasis of lines 13, 14 in cxlvii. and lines 13, 14 in clii. do not of necessity point to anything repellent in her features or expression : ('fair '), in both instances, probably refers more to her real, her inner nature, than to her external appearance but even if taken literally, Shakespeare's words would simply mean that having addressed her on occasions in the stereotyped complimentary phraseology of the time, calling her fair when she was really dark-haired, dark-eyed, and olive complexioned, he privately denounces his own forswearing, once that the glamour of passion has been wholly or almost wholly dissipated. Prof. Minto argues well for his theory that the 'Dark Woman' series was the outcome of a spirit of mockery or defiance of conventional mistress-sonneteering, intensified here and there into seeming vivid reality of emotion through the writer's essentially dramatic genius ; but it is hardly likely that he will gain wide support in this view, quite possible as it certainly is. With Professor Dowden we may conjecture if we do not in some measure owe 'Cleopatra' to this strange passion of Shakespeare : surely, the woman he so loved and of whom he sometimes wrote so bitterly (see especially the lines entitled 'A Woman' among the *Poems* in this volume), must have coloured many of his conceptions of women and women's ways? It seems to me a great mistake to consider the heroine of the sonnets as a woman destitute of beauty—Mr. Tyler would even have it, without the charm of a soft or pleasing voice—simply because of Shakespeare's allusion to her blackness or darkness of complexion : a black beauty, as has been pointed out by A. Hillard, was a phrase universally used to

express a brunette as late even as the age of
Queen Anne. A beautiful, certainly a fascinating
'brunette,' she must have been. The debateable
130th Sonnet must not be taken as expressive of
deficiencies in beauty and manners on the part of
Shakespeare's mistress : there, in a spirit of irony
as much as of earnestness, he wrote literal truth,
yet with a saving clause that transformed all he had
said, negatived his negatives so to speak.

On the Sonnets themselves I need not now ex-
patiate, great though the temptation may be.
Briefly it may be noted, as regards their metrical
structure, that much has been inconsiderately
written concerning the inefficiency of the Shakespearian as compared with other sonnet-forms.
The greatest of sonneteers since Shakespeare—
one, moreover, who himself seldom adopted the
model of the master-poet he so intensely admired—
declared that " conception—FUNDAMENTAL BRAIN
WORK—is what makes the difference in all the
art. . . . A Shakespearian Sonnet is better than
the most perfect in form, because Shakespeare
wrote it."   In confirmation of this dictum of
Rossetti, I quote the words of the chief living
authority on the 'sonnet,' Mr. Theodore Watts ;
who, after objecting to Mr. Mark Pattison's strange
assertion that Shakespeare's selection of the sonnet-
form was an unfortunate choice of vehicle, and
after justly referring to Sonnet cxxix (*The expense
of spirit in a waste of shame*) as the greatest in the
world, proceeds—" The quest of the Shakespearian
sonnet is not, like that of the form adopted by
Milton, sonority and, so to speak, metrical counter-

point, but <u>sweetness</u> ; and the sweetest of all
possible arrangements in English versification is a
succession of decasyllabic quatrains in alternate
rhymes knit together, and clinched by a couplet—a
couplet coming not too far from the initial verse
to lose its binding power, and yet not too near the
initial verse for the ring of epigram to disturb the
'linkèd sweetness long drawn out' of this move-
ment, but sufficiently near to shed its influence
over the poem back to the initial verse."

A word as to certain variations in the sonnet-
sequence as it appears in this volume. Concerning
textual emendations, suggestions, and interpret-
ations, the reader will find particulars in the notes
in the appendix   Here I shall only point out (1)
the omission of Nos. cliii-iv from the regular
sequence, they manifestly having nothing directly
to do therewith, and being, moreover, experimental
variations on the same theme. They will be found
further on in the volume under the title *Love's Fire.*
(2) The insertion—but without a number, so as not
to interfere with the accepted numeration—between
No. cxxxvi. and cxxxvii. of the sonnet '*Vows*' from
Love's Labour's Lost and *The Passionate Pilgrim*,
for reasons explained in the corresponding note.
(3.) The insertion—with the same precaution as to
numeration—between Nos. cxxxix. and cxl. of a
sonnet from *Love's Labour's Lost* which I have
named '*Love in Tears.*'   Mr. Palgrave prints it
in a poem of sixteen lines among the *Songs*, under
the title 'Morning Tears'—(*Love's Labour's Lost*,
Act iv. Sc. 3, ll. 26-42).   But lines 26-40 certainly
constitute a genuine sonnet, and as such I have

ventured to detach it from the two appended lines, and to place it among the recognised Sonnets. Of course its placement is purely conjectural. (See note). (4.) The double numbering in the case of the series addressed to a woman : the first numbers are those of general acceptance, the second, in brackets, indicative of each sonnet's place in this special series.

Veritably, to use Shakespeare's own phrase, these 'deep-brained sonnets' are a legacy of inestimable value.

> " *Subtle as Sphinx ; as sweet and musical*
> *As bright Apollo's lute, strung with his hair ;*
> *And when Love speaks, the voice of all the gods*
> *Make heaven drowsy with the harmony.*"

Their sonority, their grandeur, their beauty, their deep-reaching music and subtle human 'reverberations,' are ours whensoever we will : but still more may we find strength and refreshment in the great nature they reveal,—self-abnegating, loyal, reaching down from the heights of Supremity with a humility that has in it something of pathos as well as of spiritual nobility.

WILLIAM SHARP.

Songs from the Plays.

I.

COME UNTO THESE YELLOW SANDS.

(ARIEL, *invisible, playing and singing.*)

COME unto these yellow sands,
    And then take hands :
Courtsied when you have and kiss'd
    The wild waves whist,
Foot it featly here and there ;
And, sweet sprites, the burthen bear.

[*Burth.* (Echo) *dispersedly.*]   Hark, hark !

The Tempest.   Act i. Sc. 2.

II.

SEA MAGIC.

(Where should this music be ? i' the air or the earth ?
It sounds no more : and, sure, it waits upon
Some god o' the island.   Sitting on a bank,
Weeping again the king my father's wreck,
This music crept by me upon the waters,
Allaying both their fury and my passion
With its sweet air : thence I have follow'd it,
Or it hath drawn me rather.   But 'tis gone.
No, it begins again.) .

ARIEL *sings.*

FULL fathom five thy father lies ;
Of his bones are coral made,
Those are pearls that were his eyes :
Nothing of him that doth fade
But doth suffer a sea-change
Into something rich and strange.

The Tempest.   Act i. Sc. 2.

III.

NATURE'S BENISON.

(FERDINAND. *May I be bold*
To think these spirits ?
PROSPERO. *Spirits, which by mine art*
I have from their confines call'd to enact
My present fancies.)

HONOUR, riches, marriage-blessing,
Long continuance, and increasing,
Hourly joys be still upon you !
Juno sings her blessings on you.

Earth's increase, foison plenty,
Barns and garners never empty,
Vines with clustering bunches growing,
Plants with goodly burthen bowing ;

Spring come to you at the farthest
In the very end of harvest
Scarcity and want shall shun you ;
Ceres' blessing so is on you.

The Tempest.   Act iv. Sc. 1.

IV.

FAËRY JOYS.

(ARIEL *sings, while helping to attire* PROSPERO.)

WHERE the bee sucks, there lurk I:
In a cowslip's bell I lie;
There I couch when owls do cry.
On the bat's back I do fly
After summer merrily.
Merrily, merrily shall I live now
Under the blossom that hangs on the bough.

The Tempest.   Act. v. Sc. 1.

V.

THURIO'S SONG OF SYLVIA.

WHO is Sylvia? what is she,
    That all our swains commend her?
Holy, fair, and wise is she;
    The heaven such grace did lend her,
That she might admired be.

Is she kind as she is fair?
    For beauty lives with kindness,

Love doth to her eyes repair,
　To help him of his blindness,
And, being help'd, inhabits there.

Then to Sylvia let us sing,
　That Sylvia is excelling ;
She excels each mortal thing
　Upon the dull earth dwelling :
To her let us garlands bring.

The Two Gentlemen of Verona.　Act iv. Sc. 1.

VI.

LOVE.

Love like a shadow flies
　When substance love pursues ;
Pursuing that that flies,
　And flying what pursues.

The Merry Wives of Windsor.　Act iii. Sc. 2.

VII.

UNCHASTE DESIRE.

Fie on sinful fantasy !
Fie on lust and luxury !
Lust is but a bloody fire,
Kindled with unchaste desire,
 Fed in heart, whose flames aspire
As thought do blow them, higher and higher.

  The Merry Wives of Windsor. Act v. Sc. 5.

VIII.

BROKEN VOWS.

(The Moated Grange at St. Luke's.)
Enter MARIANA *and a* BOY.
BOY *sings.*
TAKE, O, take those lips away,
 That so sweetly were forsworn ;
And those eyes, the break of day,
 Lights that do mislead the morn :
But my kisses bring again, bring again ;
Seals of love, but sealed in vain, sealed in vain.

  Measure for Measure. Act iv. Sc. 2.

IX.

INCONSTANT LOVERS.

SIGH no more, ladies, sigh no more,
  Men were deceivers ever,
One foot in sea and one on shore,
  To one thing constant never:
Then sigh not so, but let them go,
  And be you blithe and bonny,
Converting all your sounds of woe
  Into Hey nonny, nonny.
Sing no more ditties, sing no moe,
  Of dumps so dull and heavy;
The fraud of men was ever so,
  Since summer first was leafy:
Then sigh not so, but let them go,
  And be you blithe and bonny,
Converting all your sounds of woe
  Into Hey nonny, nonny.

Much Ado About Nothing.   Act ii. Sc. 3.

X.

IN MEMORIAM.

(CLAUDIO, *in a church, reads by taper light.*)

DONE to death by slanderous tongues
  Was the Hero that here lies :
Death, in guerdon of her wrongs,
  Gives her fame which never dies.
So the life that died with shame
Lives in death with glorious fame.

(*Leaves the scroll on the tomb.*)

Hang thou there upon the tomb,
Praising her when I am dumb.
Now, music, sound, and sing your solemn hymn.

(*The Hymn.*)

Pardon, goddess of the night,
Those that slew thy virgin knight ;
For the which, with songs of woe,
Round about her tomb they go.
  Midnight, assist our moan ;
  Help us to sigh and groan,
    Heavily, heavily ;
  Graves, yawn and yield your dead,
  Till death be uttered,
    Heavily, heavily.
      Much Ado about Nothing.   Act v. Sc. 3.

XI.

WHITE AND RED.

("A dangerous rhyme, master, against the reason of
white and red.")

If she be made of white and red,
    Her faults will ne'er be known ;
For blushing cheeks by faults are bred,
    And fears by pale white shown :
Then if she fear, or be to blame,
    By this you shall not know,
For still her cheeks possess the same
    Which native she doth owe.

            Love's Labour's Lost.   Act. i. Sc. 2.

XII.

LOVE'S RHAPSODY.

(SCHOOLMASTER.—*What, my soul! verses?*
CURATE.—*Ay, sir, and very learned.*
SCHOOLMASTER.—*Let me hear a staff, a stanza, a*
    verse : lege domine.)

If love make me forsworn, how shall I swear to love ?
Ah, never faith could hold, if not to beauty vow'd !

Though to myself forsworn, to thee I'll faithful prove ;
  Those thoughts to me were oaks, to thee like osiers
    bow'd.
Study his bias leaves and makes his book thine eyes,
  Where all those pleasures live that art would compre-
    hend :
If knowledge be the mark, to know thee shall suffice ;
  Well learned is that tongue that well can thee commend,
All ignorant that soul that sees thee without wonder ;
  Which is to me some praise that I thy parts admire :
Thy eye Jove's lightning bears, thy voice his dreadful
    thunder,
  Which, not to anger bent, is music and sweet fire.
Celestial as thou art, O pardon love this wrong,
That sings heaven's praise with such an earthly tongue.

Love's Labour's Lost.   Act iv. Sc. 2.

XIII.

A LOVER'S LAMENT.

On a day—alack the day !—
Love, whose month is ever May,
Spied a blossom passing fair,
Playing in the wanton air :

Through the velvet leaves the wind,
All unseen, gan passage find ;
That the lover, sick to death,
Wish himself the heaven's breath.
"Air," quoth he, "thy cheeks may blow ;
Air, would I might triumph so !
But, alack, my hand is sworn
Ne'er to pluck thee from thy thorn ;
Vow, alack, for youth unmeet,
Youth so apt to pluck a sweet !
Do not call it sin in me,
That I am forsworn for thee ;
Thou for whom Jove would swear
Juno but an Ethiope were ;
And deny himself for Jove,
Turning mortal for thy love."

Love's Labour's Lost.   Act iv. Sc. 3.

XIV.

SPRING.

When daisies pied and violets blue,
  And lady-smocks all silver-white,
And cuckoo-buds of yellow hue
  Do paint the meadows with delight,

The cuckoo then, on every tree,
Mocks married men ; for thus sings he,
                      Cuckoo ;
Cuckoo, cuckoo : O word of fear,
Unpleasing to a married ear !

When shepherds pipe on oaten straws
  And merry larks are ploughmen's clocks,
When turtles tread, and rooks, and daws,
  And maidens bleach their summer smocks,
The cuckoo then, on every tree,
Mocks married men ; for thus sings he,
                      Cuckoo ;
Cuckoo, cuckoo : O word of fear,
Unpleasing to a married ear !

Love's Labour's Lost.   Act iv. Sc. 2.

XV.

WINTER.

WHEN icicles hang by the wall,
  And Dick the shepherd blows his nail
And Tom bears logs into the hall,
  And milk comes frozen home in pail ;

When blood is nipp'd and ways be foul,
Then nightly sings the staring owl,
                        Tu-whit:
Tu-who, a merry note,
While greasy Joan doth keel the pot.

When all aloud the wind doth blow,
    And coughing drowns the parson's saw,
And birds sit brooding in the snow,
    And Marian's nose looks red and raw,
When roasted crabs hiss in the bowl,
Then nightly sings the staring owl,
                        Tu-whit;
Tu-who, a merry note,
While greasy Joan doth keel the pot.

                 Love's Labour's Lost.   Act v. Sc. 2.

XVI.

THE ELFIN LIFE.   (1.)

(PUCK.—*How now, spirit! whither wander you?*)

Fairy.—Over hill, over dale,
        Thorough bush, thorough brier,
Over park, over pale,
        Thorough flood, thorough fire,

I do wander everywhere,
Swifter than the moon's sphere;
And I serve the fairy queen,
To dew her orbs upon the green.
The cowslips tall her pensioners be:
In their gold coats spots you see;
Those be rubies, fairy favours,
In those freckles live their savours:
I must go seek some dewdrops here,
And hang a pearl in every cowslip's ear.

A Midsummer-Night's Dream.   Act ii. Sc. 1.

XVII.

ELFIN MUSIC.

(*The Fairies sing.*)

You spotted snakes with double tongue,
  Thorny hedgehogs, be not seen;
Newts and blind-worms, do no wrong,
  Come not near our fairy queen.
Philomel, with melody
Sing in our sweet lullaby;
Lulla, lulla, lullaby, lulla, lulla, lullaby:

Never harm,
Nor spell nor charm,
Come our lovely lady nigh ;
So, good-night, with lullaby.
Weaving spiders, come not here ;
Hence, you long-legg'd spinners, hence !
Beetles black, approach not near ;
Worm nor snail, do no offence.
Philomel, with melody
Sing in our sweet lullaby ;
Lulla, lulla, lullaby, lulla, lulla, lullaby.
A Fairy—Hence, away ! now all is well :
One aloof stand sentinel.   (*Titania sleeps.*)

A Midsummer-Night's Dream.   Act ii. Sc. 2.

XVIII.

THE WOODLAND CHOIR.

THE ousel-cock so black of hue,
With orange-tawny bill,
The throstle with his note so true,
The wren with little quill,

The finch, the sparrow, and the lark ;
  The plain-song cuckoo gray,
Whose note full many a man doth mark,
  And dares not answer nay.

    A Midsummer-Night's Dream.   Act iii. Sc. 1.

XIX.

THE ELFIN LIFE. (II.)

(PUCK, *softly*.)

Now the hungry lion roars,
  And the wolf behowls the moon ;
Whilst the heavy ploughman snores,
  All with weary task fordone.
Now the wasted brands do glow,
  While the screech-owl, screeching loud,
Puts the wretch that lies in woe
  In remembrance of a shroud.
Now it is the time of night
  That the graves all gaping wide,
Everyone lets forth his sprite,
  In the church-way paths to glide :
And we fairies, that do run
  By the triple Hecate's team,

From the presence of the sun,
  Following darkness like a dream,
  Now are frolic : not a mouse
  Shall disturb this hallow'd house :
  I am sent with broom before,
  To sweep the dust behind the door.
(Oberon and Titania, with Elfin train, enter the room.)

Through the house give glimmering light,
  By the dead and drowsy fire :
  Every elf and fairy sprite
  Hop as light as bird from brier ;
  And this ditty, after me,
  Sing, and dance it trippingly.
Tit. First, rehearse your song by rote.
  To each word a warbling note :
  Hand in hand, with fairy grace,
  Will we sing, and bless this place.

(Sing and dance.)

A Midsummer-Night's Dream.   Act v. Sc. 1.

XX.

VANITAS.

SOME there be that shadows kiss;
Such have but a shadow's bliss.

XXI.

SONG.

(*Music, whilst* BASSANIO *comments on the caskets.*)

TELL me where is fancy bred,
Or in the heart or in the head ?
  How begot, how nourished ?
      Reply, reply.
It is engender'd in the eyes,
With gazing fed : and fancy dies
In the cradle where it lies.
    Let us all ring fancy's knell :
    I'll begin it,—Ding, dong, bell.
        Ding, dong, bell.

The Merchant of Venice.   Acts ii. and iii.

XXII.

FOREST JOYS.

UNDER the greenwood tree
Who loves to lie with me,
And turn his merry note
Unto the sweet bird's throat,
Come hither, come hither, come hither:
Here shall he see
No enemy
But winter and rough weather.

Who doth ambition shun
And loves to live i' the sun,
Seeking the food he eats
And pleased with what he gets,
Come hither, come hither, come hither:
Here shall he see
No enemy
But winter and rough weather.

As You Like It.   Act ii. Sc. 5.

XXIII.

INGRATITUDE.

BLOW, blow, thou winter wind,
Thou art not so unkind
　　As man's ingratitude ;
Thy tooth is not so keen
Because thou art not seen,
　　Although thy breath be rude.
Heigh-ho ! sing, heigh-ho ! unto the green holly :
Most friendship is feigning, most loving mere folly :
　　Then, heigh-ho, the holly !
　　This life is most jolly.

Freeze, freeze, thou bitter sky,
That dost not bite so nigh
　　As benefits forgot :
Though thou the waters warp,
Thy sting is not so sharp
　　As friend remember'd not.
Heigh-ho ! sing, heigh-ho ! unto the green holly :
Most friendship is feigning, most loving mere folly :
　　Then heigh-ho, the holly !
　　This life is most jolly.

As You Like It.　Act ii. Sc. 7.

XXIV.

LOVE'S PRIME.

It was a lover and his lass,
    With a hey, and a ho, and a hey nonino,
That o'er the green corn-field did pass
    In the spring time, the only pretty ring time,
When birds do sing, hey ding a ding, ding:
Sweet lovers love the spring.

Between the acres of the rye,
    With a hey, and a ho, and a hey nonino,
These pretty country folks would lie,
    In spring time, etc.

This carol they began that hour,
    With a hey, and a ho, and a hey nonino,
How that a life was but a flower
    In spring time, etc.

And therefore take the present time,
    With a hey, and a ho, and a hey nonino;
For love is crowned with the prime
    In spring time, etc.

As You Like It.   Act v. Sc. 2.

XXV.

THE MARRIAGE SONG.

(*Still Music.*   Hymen *loquitur.*)

Then is there mirth in heaven,
When earthly things made even
    Atone together.
Good duke, receive thy daughter :
Hymen from heaven brought her,
    Yea, brought her hither,
That thou might'st join her hand with his
Whose heart within his bosom is.

.   .   .   .   .   .

Peace, ho ! I bar confusion :
'Tis I must make conclusion
    Of these most strange events :
Here's eight that must take hands
To join in Hymen's bands,
    If truth holds true contents.

    You and you no cross shall part :
    You and you are heart in heart :
    You to his love must accord,
    Or have a woman to your lord :

You and you are sure together,
As the winter to foul weather.
Whiles a wedlock-hymn we sing,
Feed yourselves with questioning ;
That reason wonder may diminish,
How thus we met, and these things finish.

SONG.

Wedding is great Juno's crown :
    O blessed bond of board and bed !
Tis Hymen peoples every town ;
    High wedlock then be honoured :
Honour, high honour and renown,
To Hymen, god of every town !

As You Like It.   Act v. Sc. 4.

XXVI.

ONE IN TEN.

WAS this fair face the cause, quoth she,
    Why the Grecians sacked Troy ?
Fond done, done fond,
    Was this King Priam's joy ?

With that she sighèd as she stood,
With that she sighèd as she stood,
  And gave this sentence then ;
Among nine bad if one be good,
Among nine bad if one be good,
  There's yet one good in ten.
           All's Well that Ends Well.   Act i. Sc. 3.

XXVII.

SWEET AND TWENTY.

O MISTRESS mine, where are you roaming ?
O, stay and hear ; your true love's coming,
  That can sing both high and low :
Trip no further, pretty sweeting ;
Journeys end in lovers meeting,
  Every wise man's son doth know.

What is love ? 'tis not hereafter ;
Present mirth hath present laughter ;
  What's to come is still unsure :
In delay there lies no plenty ;
Then come kiss me, sweet and twenty,
  Youth's a stuff will not endure.
           Twelfth Night.   Act ii. Sc. 3.

XXVIII.

A LOVER'S LAMENT.

COME away, come away, death,
  And in sad cypress let me be laid ;
Fly away, fly away, breath ;
  I am slain by a fair cruel maid.
My shroud of white, stuck all with yew,
      O, prepare it !
My part of death, no one so true
      Did share it.

Not a flower, not a flower sweet,
  On my black coffin let there be strown ;
Not a friend, not a friend greet
  My poor corpse, where my bones shall be
    thrown :
A thousand thousand sighs to save,
      Lay me, O, where
Sad true lover never find my grave,
      To weep there !

Twelfth Night.   Act iii. Sc. 4.

XXIX.

I' THE SWEET O' THE YEAR.

WHEN daffodils begin to peer,
  With heigh ! the doxy over the dale,
Why, then comes in the sweet o' the year ;
  For the red blood reigns in the winter's pale.

The white sheet bleaching on the hedge,
  With heigh ! the sweet birds, O, how they sing !
Doth set my pugging tooth on edge ;
  For a quart of ale is a dish for a king.

The lark, that tirra-lyra chants,
  With heigh ! with heigh ! the thrush and the jay,
Are summer songs for me and my aunts,
  While we lie tumbling in the hay.

But shall I go mourn for that, my dear ?
  The pale moon shines by night :
And when I wander here and there,
  I then do most go right.

If tinkers may have leave to live,
  And bear the sow-skin budget,
Then my account I well may give,
  And in the stocks avouch it.

                    The Winter's Tale.   Act iv. Sc. 3.

XXX.

WHAT MAIDS LACK.

(Quoth the Pedlar)

LAWN as white as white as driven snow ;
Cypress black as e'er was crow ;
Gloves as sweet as damask roses ;
Masks for faces and for noses ;
Bugle bracelet, necklace amber,
Perfume for a lady's chamber ;
Golden quoifs and stomachers,
For my lads to give their dears :
Pins and poking-sticks of steel,
What maids lack from head to heel :
Come buy of me, come ; come buy, come buy ;
Buy, lads, or else your lasses cry :
Come buy.

The Winter's Tale.   Act iv. Sc. 4.

XXXI.

A MERRY BALLAD.

(AUTOLYCUS.—*This is a merry ballad, but a very pretty one.*

MOPSA.—*Let's have some merry ones.*

AUT.—*Why, this is a passing merry one and goes to the tune of " Two maids wooing a man:" there's scarce a maid westward but she sings it; 'tis in request, I can tell you.*

MOP.—*We can both sing it: if thou'lt bear a part, thou shalt hear; 'tis in three parts.*

DORCAS.—*We had the tune on't a month ago.*

AUT.—*I can bear my part; you must know 'tis my occupation; have at it with you.*)

SONG.

A. GET you hence, for I must go
  Where it fits not you to know.
   D. Whither? *M.* O, whither? *D.* Whither?
M. It becomes thy oath full well,
  Thou to me thy secrets tell.
   D. Me too, let me go thither.
M. Or thou goest to the grange or mill.
D. If to either, thou dost ill.

A. Neither. *D.* What, neither ? *A.* Neither.
D. Thou hast sworn my love to be.
M. Thou hast sworn it more to me :
Then whither goest ? say, whither ?

The Winter's Tale. Act iv. Sc. 4.

XXXII.

SWEET MUSIC.

ORPHEUS with his lute made trees,
And the mountain tops that freeze,
  Bow themselves when he did sing :
To his music plants and flowers
Ever sprung ; as sun and showers
  There had made a lasting spring.

Every thing that heard him play,
Even the billows of the sea,
  Hung their heads, and then lay by.
In sweet music is such art,
Killing-care and grief-of-heart
  Fall asleep, or hearing, die.

King Henry VIII. Act iii. Sc. 1.

XXXIII.

LOVE THE MAGICIAN.

(HELEN.—*Let thy song be love : this love will undo us all.
O Cupid, Cupid, Cupid !*)

LOVE, Love, nothing but love, still more !
 For, O, Love's bow
 Shoots buck and doe :
 The shaft confounds,
 Not that it wounds,
But tickles still the sore.
These lovers cry Oh ! oh ! they die !
 Yet that which seems the wound to kill,
Doth turn oh ! oh ! to ha ! ha ! he !
 So dying love lives still :
Oh ! oh ! awhile, but ha ! ha ! ha !
Oh ! oh ! groans out for ha ! ha ! ha !
 Heigh-ho !

Troilus and Cressida. Act iii. Sc. 1

XXXIV.

DOUBT NOT.

Doubt thou the stars are fire ;
Doubt that the sun doth move ;
Doubt truth to be a liar ;
But never doubt I love.

Hamlet.   Act iii. Sc. 2.

XXXV.

DEAD AND GONE.

(OPHELIA *sings.*)

How should I your true love know
    From another one ?
By his cockle hat and staff,
    And his sandal shoon.

He is dead and gone, lady,
    He is dead and gone ;
At his head a grass-green turf,
    At his heels a stone.

White his shroud as the mountain snow,
　Larded with sweet flowers ;
Which bewept to the grave did go
　With true-love showers.

And will he not come again ?
And will he not come again ?
　No, no, he is dead :
　Go to thy death-bed :
He never will come again.

His beard was as white as snow,
All flaxen was his poll :
He is gone, he is gone,
And we cast away moan :
God ha' mercy on his soul !

Hamlet.　Act iv. Sc. 4

XXXVI.

SOLDIER'S SONG.

(CASSIO.—*'Fore God, an excellent song.*
IAGO.—*I learned it in England, where, indeed, they
are most potent in potting : your Dane, your Ger-
man, and your swag-bellied Hollander—Drink,
ho !—are nothing to your English.*)

AND let me the canakin clink, clink ;
And let me the canakin clink :
   A soldier's a man ;
   A life's but a span ;
Why, then, let a soldier drink.

King Stephen was a worthy peer,
His breeches cost him but a crown ;
He held them sixpence all too dear,
With that he call'd the tailor lown.

He was a wight of high renown,
And thou art but of low degree :
'Tis pride that pulls the country down ;
Then take thine auld cloak about thee.

Othello. Act ii. Sc. 3.

XXXVII.

HARK ! HARK ! THE LARK !

(" *A wonderful sweet air, with admirable rich words*
to it.")

HARK ! hark ! the lark at heaven's gate sings,
   And Phœbus 'gins arise,
His steeds to water at those springs
   On chaliced flowers that lies ;
And winking Mary-buds begin
   To ope their golden eyes :
With every thing that pretty is,
   My lady sweet, arise :
      Arise, arise.

Cymbeline.   Act ii. Sc. 3.

XXXVIII.

FEAR NO MORE.

FEAR no more the heat o' the sun,
   Nor the furious winter's rages ;
Thou thy worldly task hast done,
   Home art gone, and ta'en thy wages :
Golden lads and girls all must,
As chimney-sweepers, come to dust.

Fear no more the frown o' the great ;
  Thou art past the tyrant's stroke ;
Care no more to clothe and eat ;
  To thee the reed is as the oak :
The sceptre, learning, physic, must
All follow this, and come to dust.

Fear no more the lightning-flash,
  Nor the all-dreaded thunder stone ;
Fear not slander, censure rash ;
  Thou hast finish'd joy and moan :
All lovers young, all lovers must
Consign to thee, and come to dust.

No exorciser harm thee !
Nor no witchcraft charm thee !
Ghost unlaid forbear thee !
Nothing ill come near thee !
Quiet consummation have ;
And renowned be thy grave !

Cymbeline.   Act iv. Sc. 2.

TO THE ONLIE BEGETTER OF
THESE INSUING SONNETS
MR. W. H. ALL HAPPINESSE
AND THAT ETERNITIE
PROMISED BY
OUR EVER-LIVING POET
WISHETH
THE WELL-WISHING
ADVENTURER IN
SETTING
FORTH
                    T. T.

Sonnets.

I

From fairest creatures we desire increase,
That thereby beauty's rose might never die,
But as the riper should by time decease,
His tender heir might bear his memory:
But thou, contracted to thine own bright eyes,
Feed'st thy light's flame with self-substantial fuel,
Making a famine where abundance lies,
Thyself thy foe, to thy sweet self too cruel.
Thou that art now the world's fresh ornament
And only herald to the gaudy spring,
Within thine own bud buriest thy content
And, tender churl, makest waste in niggarding.
 Pity the world, or else this glutton be,
 To eat the world's due, by the grave and thee.

II.

When forty winters shall besiege thy brow,
And dig deep trenches in thy beauty's field,
Thy youth's proud livery, so gazed on now,
Will be a tatter'd weed, of small worth held;
Then being ask'd where all thy beauty lies,
Where all the treasure of thy lusty days,
To say,· within thine own deep-sunken eyes,
Were an all-eating shame and thriftless praise.
How much more praise deserved thy beauty's use,
If thou couldst answer, "This fair child of mine
Shall sum my count and make my old excuse,"
Proving his beauty by succession thine !
   This were to be new made when thou art old,
   And see thy blood warm when thou feel'st it cold.

III.

Look in thy glass, and tell the face thou viewest
Now is the time that face should form another;
Whose fresh repair if now thou not renewest,
Thou dost beguile the world, unbless some mother.
For where is she so fair whose unear'd womb
Disdains the tillage of thy husbandry?
Or who is he so fond will be the tomb
Of his self-love, to stop posterity?
Thou art thy mother's glass, and she in thee
Calls back the lovely April of her prime:
So thou through windows of thine age shalt see
Despite of wrinkles this thy golden time.
    But if thou live, remember'd not to be,
    Die single, and thine image dies with thee.

IV.

UNTHRIFTY loveliness, why dost thou spend
Upon thyself thy beauty's legacy?
Nature's bequest gives nothing but doth lend,
And being frank she lends to those are free.
Then, beauteous niggard, why doth thou abuse
The bounteous largess given thee to give?
Profitless usurer, why dost thou use
So great a sum of sums, yet canst not live?
For having traffic with thyself alone,
Thou of thyself thy sweet self dost deceive.
Then how, when Nature calls thee to be gone,
What acceptable audit canst thou leave?
    Thy unused beauty must be tomb'd with thee,
    Which, used, lives th' executor to be.

V.

Those hours, that with gentle work did frame
The lovely gaze where every eye doth dwell,
Will play the tyrants to the very same
And that unfair which fairly doth excel ;
For never-resting time leads summer on
To hideous winter and confounds him there ;
Sap check'd with frost and lusty leaves quite goue,
Beauty o'ersnow'd and bareness every where :
Then, were not summer's distillation left,
A liquid prisoner pent in walls of glass,
Beauty's effect with beauty were bereft,
Nor it nor no remembrance what it was :
   But flowers distill'd, though they with winter meet,
   Leese but their show ; their substance still lives sweet.

VI.

Then let not winter's ragged hand deface
In thee thy summer, ere thou be distill'd :
Make sweet some vial ; treasure thou some place
With beauty's treasure, ere it be self-kill'd.
That use is not forbidden usury
Which happies those that pay the willing loan ;
That's for thyself to breed another thee,
Or ten times happier, be it ten for one !
Ten times thyself were happier than thou art,
If ten of thine ten times refigured thee :
Then what could death do, if thou shouldst depart,
Leaving thee living in posterity ?
    Be not self-will'd, for thou art much too fair
    To be death's conquest and make worms thine heir.

VII.

Lo ! in the orient when the gracious light
Lifts up his burning head, each under eye
Doth homage to his new-appearing sight,
Serving with looks his sacred majesty ;
And having climb'd the steep-up heavenly hill,
Resembling strong youth in his middle age,
Yet mortal looks adore his beauty still,
Attending on his golden pilgrimage ;
But when from highmost pitch, with weary car,
Like feeble age, he reeleth from the day,
The eyes, 'fore duteous, now converted are
From his low tract and look another way :
   So thou, thyself out-going in thy noon,
   Unlook'd on diest, unless thou get a son.

VIII.

Music to hear, why hear'st thou music sadly ?
Sweets with sweets war not, joy delights in joy.
Why lov'st thou that which thou receiv'st not gladly,
Or else receivest with pleasure thine annoy ?
If the true concord of well-tuned sounds,
By unions married, do offend thine ear,
They do but sweetly chide thee, who confounds
In singleness the parts that thou shouldst bear.
Mark how one string, sweet husband to another,
Strikes each in each by mutual ordering,
Resembling sire and child and happy mother
Who all in one, one pleasing note do sing :
  Whose speechless song, being many, seeming one,
  Sings this to thee : " thou single wilt prove none."

IX.

Is it for fear to wet a widow's eye
That thou consumest thyself in single life?
Ah! if thou issueless shalt hap to die,
The world will wail thee, like a makeless wife;
The world will be thy widow and still weep
That thou no form of thee hast left behind,
When every private widow well may keep
By children's eyes her husband's shape in mind.
Look, what an unthrift in the world doth spend,
Shifts but his place, for still the world enjoys it;
But beauty's waste hath in the world an end,
And kept unused, the user so destroys it.
  No love toward others in that bosom sits
  That on himself such murderous shame commits.

X.

For shame ! deny that thou bear'st love to any,
Who for thyself art so unprovident.
Grant, if thou wilt, thou art beloved of many,
But that thou none lov'st is most evident;
For thou art so possess'd with murderous hate
That 'gainst thyself thou stick'st not to conspire,
Seeking that beauteous roof to ruinate
Which to repair should be thy chief desire.
O, change thy thought, that I may change my mind !
Shall hate be fairer lodged than gentle love ?
Be, as thy presence is, gracious and kind,
Or to thyself at least kind-hearted prove :
   Make thee another self, for love of me,
   That beauty still may live in thine or thee.

XI.

As fast as thou shalt wane, so fast thou growest
In one of thine, from that which thou departest;
And that fresh blood which youngly thou bestowest
Thou mayst call thine when thou from youth convertest.
Herein lives wisdom, beauty, and increase;
Without this, folly, age, and cold decay:
If all were minded so, the times should cease,
And threescore year would make the world away.
Let those whom Nature hath not made for store,
Harsh featureless and rude, barrenly perish:
Look, whom she best endow'd she gave the more;
Which bounteous gift thou shouldst in bounty cherish:
   She carved thee for her seal, and meant thereby
   Thou shouldst print more, nor let that copy die.

XII.

When I do count the clock that tells the time,
And see the brave day sunk in hideous night;
When I behold the violet past prime,
And sable curls all silver'd o'er with white;
When lofty trees I see barren of leaves
Which erst from heat did canopy the herd,
And summer's green all girded up in sheaves
Borne on the bier with white and bristly beard,
Then of thy beauty do I question make,
That thou among the wastes of time must go,
Since sweets and beauties do themselves forsake
And die as fast as they see others grow;
   And nothing 'gainst Time's scythe can make defence
   Save breed, to brave him when he takes thee hence.

XIII.

O, THAT you were yourself! but, love, you are
No longer yours than you yourself here live:
Against this coming end you should prepare,
And your sweet semblance to some other give.
So should that beauty which you hold in lease
Find no determination; then you were
Yourself again after yourself's decease,
When your sweet issue your sweet form should bear.
Who lets so fair a house fall to decay,
Which husbandry in honour might uphold
Against the stormy gusts of winter's day
And barren rage of death's eternal cold?
   O, none but unthrifts! Dear my love, you know
   You had a father: let your son say so.

XIV.

Nor from the stars do I my judgment pluck;
And yet methinks I have astronomy,
But not to tell of good or evil luck,
Of plagues, of dearths, or seasons' quality;
Nor can I fortune to brief minutes tell,
Pointing to each his thunder, rain, and wind,
Or say with princes if it shall go well,
By oft predict that I in heaven find:
But from thine eyes my knowledge I derive,
And, constant stars, in them I read such art
As "Truth and beauty shall together thrive,
If from thyself to store thou wouldst convert;"
   Or else of thee this I prognosticate:
   "Thy end is truth's and beauty's doom and date."

XV.

When I consider every thing that grows
Holds in perfection but a little moment,
That this huge stage presenteth nought but shows
Whereon the stars in secret influence comment;
When I perceive that men as plants increase,
Cheered and check'd even by the self-same sky,
Vaunt in their youthful sap, at height decrease,
And wear their brave state out of memory;
Then the conceit of this inconstant stay
Sets you most rich in youth before my sight,
Where wasteful Time debateth with Decay,
To change your day of youth to sullied night;
 And all in war with Time for love of you,
 As he takes from you, I engraft you new.

XVI.

But wherefore do not you a mightier way
Make war upon this bloody tyrant, Time?
And fortify yourself in your decay
With means more blessed than my barren rhyme?
Now stand you on the top of happy hours,
And many maiden gardens yet unset
With virtuous wish would bear your living flowers,
Much liker than your painted counterfeit:
So should the lines of life that life repair,
Which this, Time's pencil, or my pupil pen,
Neither in inward worth nor outward fair,
Can make you live yourself in eyes of men.
    To give away yourself keeps yourself still,
    And you must live, drawn by your own sweet skill.

XVII.

Who will believe my verse in time to come,
If it were fill'd with your most high deserts?
Though yet, heaven knows, it is but as a tomb
Which hides your life and shows not half your parts.
If I could write the beauty of your eyes
And in fresh numbers number all your graces,
The age to come would say, "This poet lies;
Such heavenly touches ne'er touch'd earthly faces."
So should my papers yellow'd with their age
Be scorn'd like old men of less truth than tongue,
And your true rights be term'd a poet's rage
And stretchèd metre of an antique song:
    But were some child of yours alive that time,
    You should live twice; in it and in my rhyme.

XVIII.

Shall I compare thee to a summer's day ? ·
Thou art more lovely and more temperate :
Rough winds do shake the darling buds of May,
And summer's lease hath all too short a date :
Sometime too hot the eye of heaven shines,
And often is his gold complexion dimm'd ;
And every fair from fair sometime declines,
By chance or nature's changing course untrimm'd ;
But thy eternal summer shall not fade
Nor lose possession of that fair thou owest ;
Nor shall Death brag thou wander'st in his shade,
When in eternal lines to time thou growest ;
  So long as men can breathe or eyes can see,
    So long lives this and this gives life to thee.

XIX.

Devouring Time, blunt thou the lion's paws,
And make the earth devour her own sweet brood ;
Pluck the keen teeth from the fierce tiger's jaws,
And burn the long-lived phœnix in her blood ;
Make glad and sorry seasons as thou fleets,
And do whate'er thou wilt, swift-footed Time,
To the wide world and all her fading sweets ;
But I forbid thee one most heinous crime :
O, carve not with thy hours my love's fair brow,
Nor draw no lines there with thine antique pen ;
Him in thy course untainted do allow
For beauty's pattern to succeeding men.
    Yet, do thy worst, old Time : despite thy wrong,
    My love shall in my verse ever live young.

XX.

A WOMAN's face with Nature's own hand painted
Hast thou, the master-mistress of my passion ;
A woman's gentle heart, but not acquainted
With shifting change, as is false women's fashion ;
An eye more bright than theirs, less false in rolling,
Gilding the object whereupon it gazeth ;
A man in hue, all ' hues ' in his controlling,
Which steals men's eyes and women's souls amazeth.
And for a woman wert thou first created ;
Till Nature, as she wrought thee, fell a-doting,
And by addition me of thee defeated,
By adding one thing to my purpose nothing.
   But since she prick'd thee out for women's pleasure,
   Mine be thy love and thy love's use their treasure.

XXI.

So is it not with me as with that Muse
Stirr'd by a painted beauty to his verse,
Who heaven itself for ornament doth use
And every fair with his fair doth rehearse ;
Making a complement of proud compare,
With sun and moon, with earth and sea's rich gems,
With April's first-born flowers, and all things rare
That heaven's air in this huge rondure hems.
O, let me, true in love, but truly write,
And then believe me, my love is as fair
As any mother's child, though not so bright
As those gold candles fix'd in heaven's air :
    Let them say more that like of hearsay well ;
    I will not praise that purpose not to sell.

XXII.

My glass shall not persuade me I am old,
So long as youth and thou are of one date ;
But when in thee time's furrows I behold,
Then look I death my days should expiate.
For all that beauty that doth cover thee
Is but the seemly raiment of my heart,
Which in thy breast doth live, as thine in me :
How can I then be elder than thou art ?
O, therefore, love, be of thyself so wary
As I, not for myself, but for thee will ;
Bearing thy heart, which I will keep so chary
As tender nurse her babe from faring ill.
      Presume not on thy heart when mine is slain ;
      Thou gavest me thine, not to give back again.

XXIII.

As an unperfect actor on the stage
Who with his fear is put besides his part,
Or some fierce thing replete with too much rage,
Whose strength's abundance weakens his own heart,
So I, for fear of trust, forget to say
The perfect ceremony of love's rite,
And in mine own love's strength seem to decay,
O'ercharg'd with burden of mine own love's might.
O, let my books be then the eloquence
And dumb presages of my speaking breast,
Who plead for love and look for recompense
More than that tongue that more hath more express'd.
  O, learn to read what silent love hath writ:
  To hear with eyes belongs to love's fine wit.

XXIV.

MINE eye hath play'd the painter and hath stell'd
Thy beauty's form in table of my heart;
My body is the frame wherein 'tis held,
And perspective it is best painter's art.
For through the painter must you see his skill,
To find where your true image pictured lies;
Which in my bosom's shop is hanging still,
That hath his windows glazèd with thine eyes.
Now see what good turns eyes for eyes have done;
Mine eyes have drawn thy shape, and thine for me
Are windows to my breast, where-through the sun
Delights to peep, to gaze therein on thee;
   Yet eyes this cunning want to grace their art:
   They draw but what they see, know not the heart.

XXV.

Let those who are in favour with their stars
Of public honour and proud titles boast,
Whilst I, whom fortune of such triumph bars,
Unlook'd for joy in that I honour most.
Great princes' favourites their fair leaves spread
But as the marigold at the sun's eye,
And in themselves their pride lies buried,
For at a frown they in their glory die.
The painful warrior famousèd for fight,
After a thousand victories once foil'd,
Is from the book of honour razèd quite,
And all the rest forgot for which he toil'd:
    Then happy I, that love and am beloved
    Where I may not remove nor be removed.

XXVI.

LORD of my love, to whom in vassalage
Thy merit hath my duty strongly knit,
To thee I send this written embassage,
To witness duty, not to show my wit:
Duty so great, which wit so poor as mine
May make seem bare, in wanting words to show it,
But that I hope some good conceit of thine
In thy soul's thought, all naked, will bestow it;
Till whatsoever star that guides my moving
Points on me graciously with fair aspect,
And puts apparel on my tatter'd loving,
To show me worthy of thy sweet respect;
   Then may I dare to boast how I do love thee:
   Till then not show my head where thou may'st
     prove me.

XXVII.

WEARY with toil, I haste me to my bed,
The dear repose for limbs with travel tired ;
But then begins a journey in my head,
To work my mind, when body's work's expired ;
For then my thoughts, from far where I abide,
Intend a zealous pilgrimage to thee,
And keep my drooping eyelids open wide,
Looking on darkness which the blind do see ;
Save that my soul's imaginary sight
Presents thy shadow to my sightless view,
Which, like a jewel hung in ghastly night,
Makes black night beauteous and her old face new.
    Lo ! thus, by day my limbs, by night my mind,
    For thee and for myself no quiet find.

XXVIII.

How can I then return in happy plight,
That am debarr'd the benefit of rest ?
When day's oppression is not eased by night,
But day by night, and night by day, oppress'd ?
And each, though enemies to either's reign,
Do in consent shake hands to torture me ;
The one by toil, the other to complain
How far I toil, still farther off from thee.
I tell the day, to please him thou art bright
And dost him grace when clouds do blot the heaven :
So flatter I the swart-complexion'd night,
When sparkling stars twire not thou gild'st the even.
  But day doth daily draw my sorrows longer,
   And night doth nightly make grief's strength seem
    stronger.

XXIX.

WHEN, in disgrace with fortune and men's eyes,
I all alone beweep my outcast state,
And trouble deaf heaven with my bootless cries,
And look upon myself and curse my fate,
Wishing me like to one more rich in hope,
Featured like him, like him with friends possess'd,
Desiring this man's art and that man's scope,
With what I most enjoy contented least;
Yet in these thoughts myself almost despising,
Haply I think on thee, and then my state,
Like to the lark at break of day arising
From sullen earth, sings hymns at heaven's gate;
   For thy sweet love remember'd such wealth brings
   That then I scorn to change my state with kings.

XXX.

WHEN to the sessions of sweet silent thought
I summon up remembrance of things past,
I sigh the lack of many a thing I sought,
And with old woes new wail my dear time's waste;
Then can I drown an eye, unused to flow,
For precious friends hid in death's dateless night,
And weep afresh love's long since cancell'd woe,
And moan the expense of many a vanish'd sight:
Then can I grieve at grievances foregone,
And heavily from woe to woe tell o'er
The sad account of fore-bemoaned moan,
Which I new pay as if not paid before.
　　But if the while I think on thee, dear friend,
　　All losses are restored and sorrows end.

XXXI.

THY bosom is endeared with all hearts,
Which I by lacking have supposed dead,
And there reigns love and all love's loving parts,
And all those friends which I thought buried.
How many a holy and obsequious tear
Hath dear religious love stol'n from mine eye
As interest of the dead, which now appear
But things removed that hidden in thee lie !
Thou art the grave where buried love doth live,
Hung with the trophies of my lovers gone,
Who all their parts of me to thee did give ;
That due of many now is thine alone :
    Their images I loved I view in thee,
    And thou, all they, hast all the all of me.

XXXII.

IF thou survive my well-contented day,
When that churl Death my bones with dust shall cover,
And shalt by fortune once more re-survey
These poor rude lines of thy deceased lover,
Compare them with the bettering of the time,
And though they be outstripp'd by every pen,
Reserve them for my love, not for their rhyme,
Exceeded by the height of happier men.
O, then vouchsafe me but this loving thought:
"Had my friend's Muse grown with this growing age,
A dearer birth than this his love had brought,
To march in ranks of better equipage:
   But since he died and poets better prove,
   Theirs for their style I'll read, his for his love."

XXXIII.

FULL many a glorious morning have I seen
Flatter the mountain-tops with sovereign eye,
Kissing with golden face the meadows green,
Gilding pale streams with heavenly alchemy;
Anon permit the basest clouds to ride
With ugly rack on his celestial face,
And from the forlorn world his visage hide,
Stealing unseen to west with this disgrace:
Even so my sun one early morn did shine
With all-triumphant splendour on my brow;
But out, alack! he was but one hour mine;
The region cloud hath mask'd him from me now.
    Yet him for this my love no whit disdaineth;
    Suns of the world may stain when heaven's sun
        staineth.

XXXIV.

WHY didst thou promise such a beauteous day
And make me travel forth without my cloak,
To let base clouds o'ertake me in my way,
Hiding thy bravery in their rotten smoke?
'Tis not enough that through the cloud thou break,
To dry the rain on my storm-beaten face,
For no man well of such a salve can speak
That heals the wound and cures not the disgrace:
Nor can thy shame give physic to my grief;
Though thou repent, yet I have still the loss:
The offender's sorrow lends but weak relief
To him that bears the strong offence's cross.
   Ah! but those tears are pearl which thy love sheds,
   And they are rich and ransom all ill deeds.

XXXV.

No more be grieved at that which thou hast done :
Roses have thorns, and silver fountains mud ;
Clouds and eclipses stain both moon and sun,
And loathsome canker lives in sweetest bud.
All men make faults, and even I in this,
Authorising thy trespass with compare,
Myself corrupting, salving thy amiss,
Excusing thy sins more than thy sins are ;
For to thy sensual fault I bring in sense—
Thy adverse party is thy advocate—
And 'gainst myself a lawful plea commence :
Such civil war is in my love and hate
    That I an accessary needs must be
    To that sweet thief which sourly robs from me.

XXXVI.

Let me confess that we two must be twain,
Although our undivided loves are one :
So shall those blots that do with me remain
Without thy help by me be borne alone.
In our two loves there is but one respect,
Though in our lives a separable spite,
Which though it alter not love's sole effect,
Yet doth it steal sweet hours from love's delight.
I may not evermore acknowledge thee,
Lest my bewailed guilt should do thee shame,
Nor thou with public kindness honour me,
Unless thou take that honour from thy name !
  But do not so ; I love thee in such sort
  As, thou being mine, mine is thy good report.

XXXVII.

As a decrepit father takes delight
To see his active child do deeds of youth,
So I, made lame by fortune's dearest spite,
Take all my comfort of thy worth and truth.
For whether beauty, birth, or wealth, or wit,
Or any of these all, or all, or more,
Entitled in thy parts do crowned sit,
I make my love engrafted to this store :
So then I am not lame, poor, nor despised,
Whilst that this shadow doth such substance give
That I in thy abundance am sufficed
And by a part of all thy glory live.
   Look, what is best, that best I wish in thee :
   This wish I have ; then ten times happy me !

XXXVIII.

How can my Muse want subject to invent,
While thou dost breathe, that pour'st into my verse
Thine own sweet argument, too excellent
For every vulgar paper to rehearse ?
O, give thyself the thanks, if aught in me
Worthy perusal stand against thy sight ;
For who's so dumb that cannot write to thee,
When thou thyself dost give invention light ?
Be thou the tenth Muse, ten times more in worth
Than those old nine which rhymers invocate ;
And he that calls on thee, let him bring forth
Eternal numbers to outlive long date,
    If my slight Muse do please these curious days—
    The pain be mine, but thine shall be the praise.

XXXIX.

O, how thy worth with manners may I sing,
When thou art all the better part of me ?
What can mine own praise to mine own self bring ?
And what is't but mine own when I praise thee ?
Even for this let us divided live,
And our dear love lose name of single one,
That by this separation I may give
That due to thee which thou deservest alone.
O absence, what a torment wouldst thou prove,
Were it not thy sour leisure gave sweet leave
To entertain the time with thoughts of love
(Which time and thoughts so sweetly doth deceive),
  And that thou teachest how to make one twain,
  By praising him here who doth hence remain !

XL.

Take all my loves, my love, yea, take them all ;
What hast thou then more than thou hadst before ?
No love, my love, that thou mayst true love call ;
All mine was thine before thou hadst this more.
Then if for my love thou my love receivest,
I cannot blame thee for my love thou usest ;
But yet be blamed, if thou thyself deceivest
By wilful taste of what thyself refusest.
I do forgive thy robbery, gentle thief,
Although thou steal thee all my property ;
And yet love knows it is a greater grief
To bear love's wrong than hate's known injury.
    Lascivious grace, in whom all ill well shows,
    Kill me with spites ; yet we must not be foes.

XLI.

THOSE petty wrongs that liberty commits,
When I am sometime absent from thy heart,
Thy beauty and thy years full well befits,
For still temptation follows where thou art.
Gentle thou art and therefore to be won,
Beauteous thou art, therefore to be assailed ;
And when a woman woos, what woman's son
Will sourly leave her till she have prevailed?
Ay me ! but yet thou mightst my seat forbear,
And chide thy beauty and thy straying youth,
Who lead thee in their riot even there
Where thou art forced to break a twofold truth,
   Hers, by thy beauty tempting her to thee,
   Thine, by thy beauty being false to me.

XLII.

THAT thou hast her, it is not all my grief,
And yet it may be said I loved her dearly :
That she hath the, is of my wailing chief,
A loss in love that touches me more nearly.
Loving offenders, thus I will excuse ye :
Thou dost love her, because thou know'st I love her ;
And for my sake even so doth she abuse me,
Suffering my friend for my sake to approve her.
If I lose thee, my loss is my love's gain,
And losing her, my friend hath found that loss ;
Both find each other, and I lose both twain,
And both for my sake lay on me this cross ;
  But here's the joy ; my friend and I are one ;
  Sweet flattery ! then she loves but me alone.

XLIII.

WHEN most I wink. then do mine eyes best see,
For all the day they view things unrespected;
But when I sleep, in dreams they look on thee,
And darkly bright are bright in dark directed.
Then thou, whose shadow shadows doth make bright,
How would thy shadow's form form happy show
To the clear day with thy much clearer light,
When to unseeing eyes thy shade shines so !
How would, I say, mine eyes be blessed made
By looking on thee in the living day,
When in dead night thy fair imperfect shade
Through heavy sleep on sightless eyes doth stay !
   All days are nights to me till I see thee,
    And nights bright days when dreams do show
      thee me.

XLIV.

IF the dull substance of my flesh were thought,
Injurious distance should not stop my way;
For then despite of space I would be brought,
From limits far remote, where thou dost stay.
No matter then although my foot did stand
Upon the farthest earth removed from thee:
For nimble thought can jump both sea and land
As soon as think the place where he would be.
But, ah! thought kills me that I am not thought,
To leap large lengths of miles when thou art gone,
But that so much of earth and water wrought
I must attend time's leisure with my moan,
    Receiving nought by elements so slow
    But heavy tears, badges of either's woe.

XLV.

THE other two, slight air and purging fire,
Are both with thee, wherever I abide ;
The first my thought, the other my desire.
These present-absent with swift motion slide.
For when these quicker elements are gone
In tender embassy of love to thee,
My life, being made of four, with two alone
Sinks down to death, oppress'd with melancholy
Until life's composition be recured
By those swift messengers return'd from thee,
Who even but now come back again, assured
Of thy fair health, recounting it to me :
 This told, I joy ; but then no longer glad,
 I send them back again, and straight grow sad.

XLVI.

Mine eye and heart are at a mortal war
How to divide the conquest of thy sight ;
Mine eye my heart thy picture's sight would bar,
My heart mine eye the freedom of that right.
My heart doth plead that thou in him dost lie—
A closet never pierced with crystal eyes—
But the defendant doth that plea deny
And says in him thy fair appearance lies.
To 'cide this title is impannellèd
A quest of thoughts, all tenants to the heart,
And by their verdict is determined
The clear eye's moiety and the dear heart's part :
　　As thus ; mine eye's due is thy outward part,
　　And my heart's right thy inward love of heart.

XLVII.

BETWIXT mine eye and heart a league is took,
And each doth good turns now unto the other:
When that mine eye is famish'd for a look,
Or heart in love with sighs himself doth smother,
With my love's picture then my eye doth feast
And to the painted banquet bids my heart;
Another time mine eye is my heart's guest
And in his thoughts of love doth share a part:
So, either by thy picture or my love,
Thyself away art present still with me;
For thou not farther than my thoughts canst move,
And I am still with them and they with thee;
    Or, if they sleep, thy picture in my sight
    Awakes my heart to heart's and eye's delight.

XLVIII.

How careful was I, when I took my way,
Each trifle under truest bars to thrust,
That to my use it might unused stay
From hands of falsehood, in sure wards of trust !
But thou, to whom my jewels trifles are,
Most worthy comfort, now my greatest grief,
Thou, best of dearest and mine only care,
Art left the prey of every vulgar thief.
Thee have I not lock'd up in any chest,
Save where thou art not, though I feel thou art,
Within the gentle closure of my breast,
From whence at pleasure thou mayst come and part ;
   And even thence thou wilt be stol'n, I fear,
   For truth proves thievish for a prize so dear.

XLIX.

AGAINST that time, if ever that time come,
.Vhen I shall see thee frown on my defects,
.Vhen as thy love hath cast his utmost sum,
Call'd to that audit by advised respects ;
Against that time when thou shalt strangely pass,
And scarcely greet me with that sun, thine eye,
When love, converted from the thing it was,
Shall reasons find of settled gravity—
Against that time do I eusconce me here
Within the knowledge of mine own desert,
And this my hand against myself uprear,
To guard the lawful reasons on thy part :
   To leave poor me thou hast the strength of laws,
   Since why to love I can allege no cause.

L.

How heavy do I journey on the way,
When what I seek, my weary travel's end,
Doth teach that ease and that repose to say
' Thus far the miles are measured from thy friend !'
The beast that bears me, tired with my woe,
Plods daily on, to bear that weight in me,
As if by some instinct the wretch did know
His rider loved not speed, being made from thee :
The bloody spur cannot provoke him on
That sometimes anger thrusts into his hide ;
Which heavily he answers with a groan,
More sharp to me than spurring to his side ;
     For that same groan doth put this in my mind ;
     My grief lies onward and my joy behind.

LI.

Thus can my love excuse the slow offence
Of my dull bearer when from thee I speed :
From where thou art why should I haste me thence ?
Till I return, of posting is no need.
O, what excuse will my poor beast then find,
When swift extremity can seem but slow ?
Then should I spur, though mounted on the winds ;
In winged speed no motion shall I know :
Then can no horse with my desire keep pace ;
Therefore desire, of perfect'st love being made,
Shall neigh, no dull flesh in his fiery race ;
But love, for love, thus shall excuse my jade ;
  'Since from thee going he went wilful-slow,
    Towards thee I'll run, and give him leave to go.'

LII.

So am I as the rich, whose blessed key
Can bring him to his sweet up-lockëd treasure,
The which he will not every hour survey,
For blunting the fine point of seldom pleasure.
Therefore are feasts so solemn and so rare,
Since, seldom coming, in the long year set,
Like stones of worth they thinly placed are,
Or captain jewels in the carcanet.
So is the time that keeps you as my chest,
Or as the wardrobe which the robe doth hide,
To make some special instant special blest,
By new unfolding his imprison'd pride.
    Blessed are you, whose worthiness gives scope,
      Being had, to triumph, being lack'd, to hope.

LIII.

WHAT is your substance, whereof are you made,
That millions of strange shadows on you tend ?
Since every one hath, every one, one shade,
And you, but one, can every shadow lend.
Describe Adonis, and the counterfeit
Is poorly imitated after you :
On Helen's check all art of beauty set,
And you in Grecian tires are painted new ;
Speak of the spring and foison of the year ;
The one doth shadow of your beauty show,
The other as your bounty doth appear ;
And you in every blessed shape we know,.
   In all external grace you have some part,
   But you like none, none you, for constant heart.

LIV.

O, HOW much more doth beauty beauteous seem
By that sweet ornament which truth doth give ;
The rose looks fair, but fairer we it deem
For that sweet odour which doth in it live.
The canker-blooms have full as deep a dye
As the perfumed tincture of the roses,
Hang on such thorns and play as wantouly
When summer's breath their masked buds discloses :
But, for their virtue only is their show,
They live unwoo'd and uurespected fade,
Die to themselves.   Sweet roses do not so ;
Of their sweet deaths are sweetest odours made :
   And so of you, beauteous and lovely youth,
   When that shall fade, my verse distils your truth.

LV.

Not marble, nor the gilded monuments
Of princes, shall outlive this powerful rhyme;
But you shall shine more bright in these contents
Than unswept stone besmear'd with sluttish time.
When wasteful war shall statues overturn,
And broils root out the work of masonry,
Nor Mars his sword nor war's quick fire shall burn
The living record of your memory.
'Gainst death and all-oblivious enmity
Shall you pace forth; your praise shall still find room
Even in the eyes of all posterity
That wear this world out to the ending doom.
  So, till the judgment that yourself arise,
  You live in this, and dwell in lovers' eyes.

LVI.

Sweet love, renew thy force; be it not said
Thy edge should blunter be than appetite,
Which but to-day by feeding is allay'd,
To-morrow sharpen'd in his former might:
So, love, be thou; although to-day thou fill
Thy hungry eyes even till they wink with fulness,
To-morrow see again, and do not kill
The spirit of love with a perpetual dulness.
Let this sad interim like the ocean be
Which parts the shore, where two contracted new
Come daily to the banks, that, when they see
Return of love, more blest may be the view;
    Else call it winter, which being full of care
    Makes summer's welcome thrice more wish'd, more rare.

LVII.

BEING your slave, what should I do but tend
Upon the hours and times of your desire ?
I have no precious time at all to spend,
Nor services to do, till you require.
Nor dare I chide the world-without-end hour
Whilst I, my sovereign, watch the clock for you,
Nor think the bitterness of absence sour
When you have bid your servant once adieu ;
Nor dare I question with my jealous thought
Where you may be, or your affairs suppose,
But, like a sad slave, stay and think of nought
Save, where you are how happy you make those.
   So true a fool is love that in your Will,
   Though you do any thing, he thinks no ill.

LVIII.

THAT god forbid (that made me first your slave),
I should in thought coutrol your times of pleasure,
Or at your hand the account of hours to crave,
Being your vassal, bound to stay your leisure !
O, let me suffer, being at your beck,
The imprison'd absence of your liberty ;
And patience, tame to sufferance, bide each check,
Without accusing you of injury.
Be where you list, your charter is so strong
That you yourself may privilege your time
To what you will : to you it doth belong
Yourself to pardon of self-doing crime.
   I am to wait, though waiting so be hell ;
   Not blame your pleasure, be it ill or well.

LIX.

If there be nothing new, but that which is
Hath been before, how are our brains beguiled,
Which, labouring for invention, bear amiss
The second burthen of a former child !
O, that recòrd could with a backward look,
Even of five hundred courses of the sun,
Show me your image in some antique book,
Since mind at first in character was done !
That I might see what the old world could say
To this composed wonder of your frame ;
Whether we are mended, or whe'er better they,
Or whether revolution be the same.
   O, sure I am, the wits of former days
   To subjects worse have given admiring praise.

LX.

Like as the waves make towards the pebbled shore,
So do our minutes hasten to their end ;
Each changing place with that which goes before,
In sequent toil all forwards do contend.
Nativity, once in the main of light,
Crawls to maturity, wherewith being crown'd,
Crooked eclipses 'gainst his glory fight,
And Time that gave doth now his gift confound.
Time doth transfix the flourish set on youth
And delves the parallels in beauty's brow,
Feeds on the rarities of Nature's truth,
And nothing stands but for his scythe to mow :
   And yet to times in hope my verse shall stand,
   Praising thy worth, despite his cruel hand.

LXI.

Is it thy will thy image should keep open
My heavy eyelids to the weary night ?
Dost thou desire my slumbers should be broken,
While shadows like to thee do mock my sight ?
Is it thy spirit that thou send'st from thee
So far from home into my deeds to pry,
To find out shames and idle hours in me,
The scope and tenour of thy jealousy ?
O, no ! thy love, though much, is not so great :
It is my love that keeps mine eye awake ;
Mine own true love that doth my rest defeat,
To play the watchman ever for thy sake :
   For thee watch I whilst thou dost wake elsewhere,
   From me far off, with others all too near.

LXII.

Sin of self-love possesseth all mine eye
And all my soul and all my every part ;
And for this sin there is no remedy,
It is so grounded inward in my heart.
Methinks no face so gracious is as mine,
No shape so true, no truth of such account ;
And for myself mine own worth do define,
As I all other in all worths surmount.
But when my glass shows me myself indeed,
Beated and chopp'd with tann'd antiquity,
Mine own self-love quite contrary I read ;
Self so self-loving were iniquity.
   'Tis thee, myself, that for myself I praise,
   Painting my age with beauty of thy days.

LXIII.

AGAINST my love shall be, as I am now,
With Time's injurious hand crush'd and o'erworn ;
When hours have drain'd his blood and fill'd his brow
With lines and wrinkles ; when his youthful morn
Hath travell'd on to age's steepy night,
And all those beauties whereof now he's king
Are vanishing or vanish'd out of sight,
Stealing away the treasure of his spring ;
For such a time do I now fortify
Against confounding age's cruel knife,
That he shall never cut from memory
My sweet love's beauty, though my lover's life :
His beauty shall in these black lines be seen,
    And they shall live, aud he in them still green.

LXIV

When I have seen by Time's fell hand defaced
The rich proud cost of outworn buried age;
When sometime lofty towers I see down-razed
And brass eternal slave to mortal rage;
When I have seen the hungry ocean gain
Advantage on the kingdom of the shore,
And the firm soil win of the watery main,
Increasing store with loss and loss with store;
When I have seen such interchange of state,
Or state itself confounded to decay;
Ruin hath taught me thus to ruminate,
That time will come and take my love away.
    This thought is as a death, which cannot choose
    But weep to have that which it fears to lose.

LXV.

Since brass, nor stone, nor earth, nor boundless sea,
But sad mortality o'er-sways their power,
How with this rage shall beauty hold a plea,
Whose action is no stronger than a flower?
O, how shall summer's honey breath hold out
Against the wreckful siege of battering days,
When rocks impregnable are not so stout,
Nor gates of steel so strong, but time decays?
O fearful meditation! where, alack,
Shall Time's best jewel from Time's quest lie hid?
Or what strong hand can hold his swift foot back?
Or who his spoil of beauty can forbid?
   O, none, unless this miracle have might,
   That in black ink my love may still shine bright.

LXVI.

TIRED with all these, for restful death I cry,
As, to behold desert a beggar born,
And needy nothing trimm'd in jollity,
And purest faith unhappily forsworn,
And gilded honour shamefully misplaced,
And maiden virtue rudely strumpeted,
And right perfection wrongfully disgraced,
And strength by limping sway disabled,
And art made tongue-tied by authority,
And folly doctor-like controlling skill,
And simple truth miscall'd simplicity,
And captive good attending captain ill ;
    Tired with all these, from these would I be gone,
    Save that, to die, I leave my love alone.

LXVII.

Ah ! wherefore with infection should he live,
And with his presence grace impiety,
That sin by him advantage should achieve
And lace itself with his society ?
Why should false painting imitate his cheek
And steal dead seeming of his living hue?
Why should poor beauty indirectly seek
Roses of shadow, since his rose is true ?
Why should he live, now Nature bankrupt is,
Beggar'd of blood to blush through lively veins ?
For she hath no exchequer now but his,
And, proud of many, lives upon his gains.
   O, him she stores, to show what wealth she had
   In days long since, before these last so bad.

LXVIII.

Thus is his cheek the map of days outworn,
When beauty lived and died as flowers do now,
Before these bastard signs of fair were born,
Or durst inhabit on a living brow;
Before the golden tresses of the dead,
The right of sepulchres, were shorn away,
To live a second life on second head;
Ere beauty's dead fleece made another gay;
In him those holy antique hours are seen,
Without all ornament, itself and true,
Making no summer of another's green,
Robbing no old to dress his beauty new;
   And him as for a map doth Nature store,
   To show false Art what beauty was of yore.

LXIX.

THOSE parts of thee that the world's eye doth view
Want nothing that the thought of hearts can mend ;
All tongues, the voice of souls, give thee that due,
Uttering bare truth, even so as foes commend.
Thy outward thus with outward praise is crown'd ;
But those same tongues that give thee so thine own
In other accents do this praise confound
By seeing farther than the eye hath shown
They look into the beauty of thy mind,
And that, in guess, they measure by thy deeds ;
Then, churls, their thoughts, although their eyes were
    kind,
To thy fair flower add the rank smell of weeds :
  But why thy odour matcheth not thy show,
  The solve is this, that thou dost common grow.

LXX.

THAT thou art blamed shall not be thy defect,
For slander's mark was ever yet the fair ;
The ornament of beauty is suspect,
A crow that flies in heaven's sweetest air.
So thou be good, slander doth but approve
Thy worth the greater, being woo'd of time ;
For canker vice the sweetest buds doth love,
And thou present'st a pure unstained prime.
Thou hast pass'd by the ambush of young days,
Either not assail'd or victor being charged ;
Yet this thy praise cannot be so thy praise,
To tie up envy evermore enlarged ;
   If some suspect of ill mask'd not thy show,
   Then thou aloue kiugdoms of hearts shouldst
      owe.

LXXI.

No longer mourn for me when I am dead
Than you shall hear the surly sullen bell
Give warning to the world that I am fled
From this vile world, with vilest worms to dwell .
Nay, if you read this line, remember not
The hand that writ it ; <u>for</u> I love you so
That I in your sweet thoughts would be forgot
If thinking on me then should make you woe.
O, if, I say, you look upon this verse
When I perhaps compounded am with clay,
Do not so much as my poor name rehearse,
But let your love even with my life decay,
    Lest the wise world should look into your moan
    And mock you with me after I am gone.

LXXII.

O, LEST the world should task you to recite
What merit lived in me, that you should love
After my death, dear love, forget me quite,
For you in me can nothing worthy prove ;
Unless you would devise some virtuous lie,
To do more for me than mine own desert,
And hang more praise upon deceased I
Than niggard truth would willingly impart :
O, lest your true love may seem false in this,
That you for love speak well of me untrue,
My name be buried where my body is,
And live no more to shame nor me nor you.
  For I am shamed by that which I bring forth,
  And so should you, to love things nothing worth.

LXXIII.

THAT time of year thou mayst in me behold
When yellow leaves, or none, or few, do hang
Upon those boughs which shake against the cold,
Bare ruin'd choirs, where late the sweet birds sang.
In me thou see'st the twilight of such day
As after sunset fadeth in the west,
Which by and by black night doth take away,
Death's second self, that seals up all in rest.
In me thou see'st the glowing of such fire
That on the ashes of his youth doth lie,
As the death-bed whereon it must expire
Consumed with that which it was nourish'd by.
   This thou perceivest, which makes thy love more strong,
   To love that well which thou must leave ere long.

LXXIV.

But be contented : when that fell arrest
Without all bail shall carry me away,
My life hath in this line some interest,
Which for memorial still with thee shall stay.
When thou reviewest this, thou dost review
The very part was consecrate to thee :
The earth can have but earth, which is his due :
My spirit is thine, the better part of me :
So then thou hast but lost the dregs of life,
The prey of worms, my body being dead,
The coward conquest of a wretch's knife,
Too base of thee to be remembered.
   The worth of that is that which it contains,
   And that is this, and this with thee remains.

LXXV.

So are you to my thoughts as food to life,
Or as sweet-season'd showers are to the ground ;
And for the peace of you I hold such strife
As 'twixt a miser and his wealth is found ;
Now proud as an enjoyer and anon
Doubting the filching age will steal his treasure,
Now counting best to be with you alone,
Then better'd that the world may see my pleasure ;
Sometime all full with feasting on your sight
And by and by clean starved for a look ;
Possessing or pursuing no delight,
Save what is had or must from you be took.
    Thus do I pine and surfeit day by day,
    Or gluttoning on all, or all away.

LXXVI.

Why is my verse so barren of new pride,
So far from variation or quick change?
Why with the time do I not glance aside
To new-found methods and to compounds strange?
Why write I still all one, ever the same,
And keep invention in a noted weed,
That every word doth almost tell my name,
Showing their birth and where they did proceed?
O, know, sweet love, I always write of you,
And you and love are still my argument;
So all my best is dressing old words new,
Spending again what is already spent :
  For as the sun is daily new and old,
  So is my love still telling what is told.

LXXVII.

THY glass will show thee how thy beauties wear,
Thy dial how thy precious minutes waste :
The vacant leaves thy mind's imprint will bear,
And of this book this learning mayst thou taste.
The wrinkles which thy glass will truly show
Of mouthed graves will give thee memory ;
Thou by thy dial's shady stealth mayst know
Time's thievish progress to eternity.
Look, what thy memory can not contain
Commit to these waste blanks, and thou shalt find
Those children nursed, deliver'd from thy brain,
To take a new acquaintance of thy mind.
    These offices, so oft as thou wilt look,
    Shall profit thee and much enrich thy book.

LXXVIII.

So oft have I envoked thee for my Muse
And found such fair assistance in my verse
As every alien pen hath got my use
And under thee their poesy disperse.
Thine eyes that taught the dumb on high to sing
And heavy ignorance aloft to fly
Have added feathers to the learned's wing
And given grace a double majesty.
Yet be most proud of that which I compile,
Whose influence is thine and born of thee :
In others' works thou dost but mend the style,
And arts with thy sweet graces graced be ;
    But thou art all my art and dost advance
    As high as learning my rude ignorance.

LXXIX.

Whilst I alone did call upon thy aid,
My verse alone had all thy gentle grace,
But now my gracious numbers are decay'd
And my sick Muse doth give another place.
I grant, sweet love, thy lovely argument
Deserves the travail of a worthier pen,
Yet what of thee thy poet doth invent
He robs thee of and pays it thee again.
He lends thee virtue and he stole that word
From thy behaviour; beauty doth he give
And found it in thy cheek; he can afford
No praise to thee but what in thee doth live.
   Then thank him not for that which he doth say,
   Since what he owes thee thou thyself dost pay.

LXXX.

O, how I faint when I of you do write,
Knowing a better spirit doth use your name,
And in the praise thereof spends all his might,
To make me tongue-tied, speaking of your fame !
But since your worth, wide as the ocean is,
The humble as the proudest sail doth bear,
My saucy bark inferior far to his
On your broad main doth wilfully appear.
Your shallowest help will hold me up afloat,
Whilst he upon your soundless deep doth ride ;
Or, being wreck'd, I am a worthless boat,
He of tall building and of goodly pride :
    Then if he thrive and I be cast away,
    The worst was this ; my love was my decay.

LXXXI.

Or I shall live your epitaph to make,
Or you survive when I in earth am rotten ;
From hence your memory death cannot take,
Although in me each part will be forgotten.
Your name from hence immortal life shall have,
Though I, once gone, to all the world must die :
The earth can yield me but a common grave,
When you entombèd in men's eyes shall lie.
Your monument shall be my gentle verse,
Which eyes not yet created shall o'er-read,
And tongues to be your being shall rehearse
When all the breathers of this world are dead ;
   You still shall live—such virtue hath my pen—
   Where breath most breathes, even in the mouths
      of men.

LXXXII.

I GRANT thou wert not married to my Muse
And therefore mayst without attaint o'erlook
The dedicated words which writers use
Of their fair subject, blessing every book.
Thou art as fair in knowledge as in hue,
Finding thy worth a limit past my praise,
And therefore art enforced to seek anew
Some fresher stamp of the time-bettering days.
And do so, love ; yet when they have devised
What strained touches rhetoric can lend,
Thou truly fair wert truly sympathized
In true plain words by thy true-telling friend ;
   And their gross painting might he better used
   Where cheeks need blood ; in thee it is abused.

LXXXIII.

I NEVER saw that you did painting need,
And therefore to your fair no painting set ;
I found, or thought I found, you did exceed
The barren tender of a poet's debt ;
And therefore have I slept in your report,
That you yourself being extant well might show
How far a modern quill doth come too short,
Speaking of worth, what worth in you doth grow.
This silence for my sin you did impute,
Which shall be most my glory, being dumb ;
For I impair not beauty being mute,
When others would give life and bring a tomb.
   There lives more life in one of your fair eyes
   Than both your poets can in praise devise.

LXXXIV.

Who is it that says most? which can say more
Than this rich praise, that you alone are you?
In whose confine immured is the store
Which should example where your equal grew.
Lean penury within that pen doth dwell
That to his subject lends not some small glory;
But he that writes of you, if he can tell
That you are you, so dignifies his story,
Let him but copy what in you is writ,
Not making worse what Nature made so clear,
And such a counterpart shall fame his wit,
Making his style admired every where.
 You to your beauteous blessings add a curse,
 Being fond on praise, which makes your
  praises worse.

LXXXV.

My tongue-tied Muse in manners holds her still,
While comments of you praise, richly compiled,
Reserve their character with golden quill
And precious phrase by all the Muses filed.
I think good thoughts whilst others write good
    words,
And like unletter'd clerk still cry "Amen"
To every hymn that able spirit affords
In polish'd form of well-refined pen.
Hearing you praised, I say "'Tis so, 'tis true,"
And to the most of praise add something more:
But that is in my thought, whose love to you,
Though words come hindmost, holds his rank
    before.
  Then others for the breath of words respect,
  Me for my dumb thoughts, speaking in effect.

LXXXVI.

Was it the proud full sail of his great verse,
Bound for the prize of all to precious you,
That did my ripe thoughts in my brain inhearse,
Making their tomb the womb wherein they grew ?
Was it his spirit, by spirits taught to write
Above a mortal pitch, that struck me dead ?
No, neither he, nor his compeers by night
Giving him aid, my verse astonished.
He, nor that affable familiar ghost
Which nightly gulls him with intelligence,
As victors of my silence cannot boast ;
I was not sick of any fear from thence :
 But when your countenance fill'd up his liue,
 Then lack'd I matter ; that enfeebled mine.

LXXXVII.

FAREWELL ! thou art too dear for my possessing,
And like enough thou know'st thy estimate :
The charter of thy worth gives thee releasing ;
My bonds in thee are all determinate.
For how do I hold thee but by thy granting ?
And for that riches where is my deserving ?
The cause of this fair gift in me is wanting,
And so my patent back again is swerving.
Thyself thou gavest, thy own worth then not
    knowing,
Or me, to whom thou gavest it, else mistaking ;
So thy great gift, upon misprision growing,
Comes home again, on better judgment making.
  Thus have I had thee, as a dream doth flatter,
  In sleep a king, but waking no such matter.

LXXXVIII.

WHEN thou shalt be disposed to set me light
And place my merit in the eye of scorn,
Upon thy side again against myself I'll fight
And prove thee virtuous, though thou art forsworn.
With mine own weakness being best acquainted,
Upon thy part I can set down a story
Of faults conceal'd, wherein I am attainted,
That thou in losing me shalt win much glory :
And I by this will be a gainer too ;
For bending all my loving thoughts on thee,
The injuries that to myself I do,
Doing thee vantage, double-vantage me.
    Such is my love, to thee I so belong,
    That for thy right myself will bear all wrong.

LXXXIX.

SAY that thou didst forsake me for some fault,
And I will comment upon that offence ;
Speak of my lameness, and I straight will halt,
Against thy reasons making no defence.
Thou canst not, love, disgrace me half so ill,
To set a form 'upon desired change,
As I'll myself disgrace : knowing thy will,
I will acquaintance strangle and look strange,
Be absent from thy walks, and in my tongue
Thy sweet beloved name no more shall dwell,
Lest I, too much profane, should do it wrong
And haply of our old acquaintance tell.
   For thee against myself I'll vow debate,
   For I must ne'er love him whom thou dost hate.

XO.

THEN hate me when thou wilt; if ever, now;
Now, while the world is bent my deeds to cross,
Join with the spite of fortune, make me bow,
And do not drop in for an after-loss :
Ah, do not, when my heart hath 'scaped this sorrow,
Come in the rearward of a conquer'd woe;
Give not a windy night a rainy morrow,
To linger out a purposed overthrow.
If thou wilt leave me, do not leave me last,
When other petty griefs have done their spite,
But in the onset come; so shall I taste
At first the very worst of fortune's might,
　　And other strains of woe, which now seem woe,
　　Compared with loss of thee will not seem so.

XCI.

Some glory in their birth, some in their skill,
Some in their wealth, some in their bodies' force,
Some in their garments, though new-fangled ill,
Some in their hawks and hounds, some in their
    horse ;
And every humour hath his adjunct pleasure,
Wherein it finds a joy above the rest :
But these particulars are not my measure ;
All these I better in one general best.
Thy love is better than high birth to me,
Richer than wealth, prouder than garments' cost,
Of more delight than hawks or horses be ;
And having thee, of all men's pride I boast :
    Wretched in this alone, that thou mayst take
    All this away and me most wretched make.

XCII.

But do thy worst to steal thyself away,
For term of life thou art assured mine,
And life no longer than thy love will stay,
For it depends upon that love of thine.
Then need I not to fear the worst of wrongs,
When in the least of them my life hath end.
I see a better state to me belongs
Than that which ou thy humour doth depend ;
Thou caust not vex me with inconstant mind,
Since that my life on thy revolt doth lie.
O, what a happy title do I find,
Happy to have thy love, happy to die !
    But what's so blessed-fair that fears no blot ?
    Thou mayst be false, and yet I know it not.

XCIII.

So shall I live, supposing thou art true,
Like a deceivèd husband ; so love's face
May still seem love to me, though alter'd new ;
Thy looks with me, thy heart in other place :
For there can live no hatred in thine eye,
Therefore in that I cannot know thy change.
In many's looks the false heart's history
Is writ in moods and frowns and wrinkles strange,
But heaven in thy creation did decree
That in thy face sweet love should ever dwell ;
Whate'er thy thoughts or thy heart's workings be,
Thy looks should nothing thence but sweetness
    tell.
    How like Eve's apple doth thy beauty grow,
      If thy sweet virtue answer not thy show !

XCIV.

THEY that have power to hurt and will do none,
That do not do the thing they most do show,
Who, moving others, are themselves as stone,
Unmoved, cold, and to temptation slow,
They rightly do inherit heaven's graces
And husband Nature's riches from expense ;
They are the lords and owners of their faces,
Others but stewards of their excellence.
The summer's flower is to the summer sweet,
Though to itself it only live and die,
But if that flower with base infection meet,
The basest weed outbraves his dignity :
    For sweetest things turn sourest by their deeds ;
    Lilies that fester smell far worse than weeds.

XCV.

How sweet and lovely dost thou make the shame
Which, like a canker in the fragrant rose,
Doth spot the beauty of thy budding name!
O, in what sweets dost thou thy sins enclose!
That tongue that tells the story of thy days,
Making lascivious comments on thy sport,
Cannot dispraise but in a kind of praise;
Naming thy name blesses an ill report.
O, what a mansion have those vices got
Which for their habitation chose out thee,
Where beauty's veil doth cover every blot,
And all things turn to fair that eyes can see!
   Take heed, dear heart, of this large privilege;
   The hardest knife ill-used doth lose its edge.

XCVI.

Some say thy fault is youth, some wantonness;
Some say thy grace is youth and gentle sport;
Both grace and faults are loved of more and less;
Thou makest faults graces that to thee resort.
As on the finger of a throned queen
The basest jewel will be well esteem'd,
So are those errors that in thee are seen
To truths translated and for true things deem'd.
How many lambs might the stern wolf betray,
If like a lamb he could his looks translate!
How many gazers mightst thou lead away,
If thou wouldst use the strength of all thy state!
    But do not so; I love thee in such sort
    As, thou being mine, mine is thy good report.

XCVII.

How like a winter hath my absence been
From thee, the pleasure of the fleeting year !
What freezings have I felt, what dark days seen !
What old December's bareness every where !
And yet this time removed was summer's time,
The teeming autumn, big with rich increase,
Bearing the wanton burden of the prime,
Like widow'd wombs after their lords' decease :
Yet this abundant issue seem'd to me
But hope of orphans and unfather'd fruit ;
For summer and his pleasures wait on thee,
And, thou away, the very birds are mute ;
   Or, if they sing, 'tis with so dull a cheer
   That leaves look pale, dreading the winter's near.

XCVIII.

From you have I been absent in the spring,
When proud-pied April dress'd in all his trim
Hath put a spirit of youth in every thing,
That heavy Saturn laugh'd and leap'd with him.
Yet nor the lays of birds nor the sweet smell
Of different flowers in odour and in hue
Could make me any summer's story tell,
Or from their proud lap pluck them where they grew;
Nor did I wonder at the lily's white,
Nor praise the deep vermilion in the rose;
They were but sweet, but figures of delight,
Drawn after you, you pattern of all those.
   Yet seem'd it winter still, and, you away,
   As with your shadow I with these did play:

XCIX.

THE froward violet thus did I chide :
Sweet thief, whence didst thou steal thy sweet that
    smells,
If not from my love's breath ?   The purple pride
Which on thy soft cheek for complexion dwells
In my love's veins thou hast too grossly dyed.
The lily I condemned for thy hand,
And buds of marjoram had stol'n thy hair :
The roses fearfully on thorns did stand,
One blushing shame, another white despair ;
A third, nor red nor white, had stol'n of both
And to his robbery had annex'd thy breath ;
But, for his theft, in pride of all his growth
A vengeful canker eat him up to death.
   More flowers I noted, yet I none could see
    But sweet or colour it had stol'n from thee.

C.

WHERE art thou, Muse, that thou forget'st so long
To speak of that which gives thee all thy might?
Spend'st thou thy fury on some worthless song,
Darkening thy power to lend base subjects light?
Return, forgetful Muse, and straight redeem
In gentle numbers time so idly spent;
Sing to the ear that doth thy lays esteem
And gives thy pen both skill and argument.
Rise, resty Muse, my love's sweet face survey,
If Time have any wrinkle graven there;
If any, be a satire to decay,
And make Time's spoils despised every where.
   Give my love fame faster than Time wastes life;
   So thou prevent'st his scythe and crooked knife.

CI.

O TRUANT Muse, what shall be thy amends
For thy neglect of truth in beauty dyed?
Both truth and beauty on my love depends;
So dost thou too, and therein dignified.
Make answer, Muse: wilt thou not haply say
"Truth needs no colour, with his colour fix'd;
Beauty no pencil, beauty's truth to lay;
But best is best, if never intermix'd?"
Because he needs no praise, wilt thou be dumb?
Excuse not silence so; for't lies in thee
To make him much outlive a gilded tomb,
And to be praised of ages yet to be.
   Then do thy office, Muse; I teach thee how
   To make him seem long hence as he shows now.

CII.

My love is strengthen'd, though more weak in seeming ;
I love not less, though less the show appear :
That love is merchandized whose rich esteeming
The owner's tongue doth publish every where.
Our love was new and then but in the spring
When I was wont to greet it with my lays,
As Philomel in summer's front doth sing
And stops her pipe in growth of riper days :
Not that the summer is less pleasant now
Than when her mournful hymns did hush the night,
But that wild music burthens every bough
And sweets grown common lose their dear delight.
  Therefore like her I sometime hold my tongue,
  Because I would not dull you with my song.

CIII.

ALACK, what poverty my Muse brings forth,
That having such a scope to show her pride,
The argument all bare is of more worth
Than when it hath my added praise beside !
O, blame me not, if I no more can write !
Look in your glass, and there appears a face
That over-goes my blunt invention quite,
Dulling my lines and doing me disgrace.
Were it not sinful then, striving to mend,
To mar the subject that before was well ?
For to no other pass my verses tend
Than of your graces and your gifts to tell ;
    And more, much more, than in my verse can sit
    Your own glass shows you when you look in it.

CIV.

To me, fair friend, you never can be old,
For as you were when first your eye I eyed,
Such seems your beauty still.   Three winters cold
Have from the forests shook three summers' pride,
Three beauteous springs to yellow autumn turn'd
In process of the seasons have I seen,
Three April perfumes in three hot Junes burn'd,
Since first I saw you fresh, which yet are green.
Ah ! yet doth beauty, like a dial-hand,
Steal from his figure and no pace perceived ;
So your sweet hue, which methinks still doth stand,
Hath motion and mine eye may be deceived :
   For fear of which, hear this, thou age unbred ;
   Ere you were born was beauty's summer dead.

CV.

LET not my love be call'd idolatry,
Nor my beloved as an idol show,
Since all alike my songs and praises be
To one, of one, still such, and ever so.
Kind is my love to-day, to-morrow kind,
Still constant in a wondrous excellence ;
Therefore my verse to constancy confined,
One thing expressing, leaves out difference.
" Fair, kind, and true " is all my argument,
" Fair, kind, and true " varying to other words ;
And in this change is my invention spent,
Three themes in one, which wondrous scope
      affords.
  " Fair, kind, and true," have often lived alone,
   Which three till now never kept seat in one.

CVI.

WHEN in the chronicle of wasted time
I see descriptions of the fairest wights,
And beauty making beautiful old rhyme
In praise of ladies dead and lovely knights,
Then, in the blazon of sweet beauty's best,
Of hand, of foot, of lip, of eye, of brow,
I see their antique pen would have express'd
Even such a beauty as your master now.
So all their praises are but prophecies
Of this our time, all you prefiguring ;
And, for they look'd but with divining eyes,
They had not skill enough your worth to sing :
    For we, which now behold these present days,
    Have eyes to wonder, but lack tongues to praise.

CVII.

Not mine own fears, nor the prophetic soul
Of the wide world dreaming on things to come,
Can yet the lease of my true love control,
Supposed as forfeit to a confined doom.
The mortal moon hath her eclipse endured
And the sad augurs mock their own presage ;
Incertainties now crown themselves assured
And peace proclaims olives of endless age.
Now with the drops of this most balmy time
My love looks fresh, and death to me subscribes,
Since, spite of him, I'll live in this poor rhyme,
While he insults o'er dull and speechless tribes :
    And thou in this shalt find thy monument,
    When tyrants' crests and tombs of brass are spent.

CVIII.

WHAT's in the brain that ink may character
Which hath not figured to thee my true spirit;
What's new to speak, what new to register,
That may express my love or thy dear merit?
Nothing, sweet boy; but yet, like prayers divine,
I must each day say o'er the very same,
Counting no old thing old, thou mine, I thine,
Even as when first I hallow'd thy fair name.
So that eternal love in love's fresh case
Weighs not the dust and injury of age,
Nor gives to necessary wrinkles place,
But makes antiquity for aye his page,
  Finding the first conceit of love there bred
   Where time and outward form would show it dead.

CIX.

O, NEVER say that I was false of heart,
Though absence seem'd my flame to qualify,
As easy might I from myself depart
As from my soul, which in thy breast doth lie:
That is my home of love: if I have ranged,
Like him that travels I return again,
Just to the time, not with the time exchanged,
So that myself bring water for my stain.
Never believe, though in my nature reign'd
All frailties that besiege all kinds of blood,
That it could so preposterously be stain'd,
To leave for nothing all thy sum of good;
    For nothing this wide universe I call,
    Save thou, my rose; in it thou art my all.

CX.

Alas, 'tis true I have gone here and there
And made myself a motley to the view,
Gored mine own thoughts, sold cheap what is most
    dear,
Made old offences of affections new :
Most true it is that I have look'd on truth
Askance and strangely : but, by all above,
These blenches gave my heart another youth,
And worse essays proved thee my best of love.
Now all is done, have what shall have no end :
Mine appetite I never more will grind
On newer proof, to try an older friend,
A god in love, to whom I am confined.
    Then give me welcome, next my heaven the best,
    Even to thy pure and most most loving breast.

CXI.

O, FOR my sake do you with Fortune chide,
The guilty goddess of my harmful deeds,
That did not better for my life provide
Than public means which public manners breeds.
Thence comes it that my name receives a brand,
And almost thence my nature is subdued
To what it works in, like the dyer's hand :
Pity me then and wish I were renew'd ;
Whilst, like a willing patient, I will drink
Potions of eisel 'gainst my strong infection ;
No bitterness that I will bitter think,
Nor double penance, to correct correction.
    Pity me then, dear friend, and I assure ye
    Even that your pity is enough to cure me.

CXII.

Your love and pity doth the impression fill
Which vulgar scandal stamp'd upon my brow;
For what care I who calls me well or ill,
So you o'er-green my bad, my good allow?
You are my all the world, and I must strive
To know my shames and praises from your tongue;
None else to me, nor I to none alive,
That my steel'd sense or changes right or wrong.
In so profound abysm I throw all care
Of others' voices, that my adder's sense
To critic and to flatterer stoppèd are.
Mark how with my neglect I do dispense:
    You are so strongly in my purpose bred
    That all the world besides methinks are dead.

CXIII.

SINCE I left you, mine eye is in my mind:
And that which governs me to go about
Doth part his function and is partly blind,
Seems seeing, but effectually is out;
For it no form delivers to the heart
Of bird, of flower, or shape, which it doth latch:
Of his quick objects hath the mind no part,
Nor his own vision holds what it doth catch;
For if it see the rudest or gentlest sight,
The most sweet favour or deformed'st creature,
The mountain or the sea, the day or night,
The crow or dove, it shapes them to your feature:
    Incapable of more, replete with you,
    My most true mind thus makes mine eye untrue.

CXIV.

On whether doth my mind, being crown'd with you,
Drink up the monarch's plague, this flattery?
Or whether shall I say, mine eye saith true,
And that your love taught it this alchemy,
To make of monsters and things indigest
Such cherubins as your sweet self resemble,
Creating every bad a perfect best,
As fast as objects to his beams assemble?
O, 'tis the first; 'tis flattery in my seeing,
And my great mind most kingly drinks it up:
Mine eye well knows what with his gust is 'grecing,
And to his palate doth prepare the cup:
 If it be poison'd, 'tis the lesser sin
 That mine eye loves it and doth first begin.

CXV.

Those lines that I before have writ do lie,
Even those that said I could not love you dearer:
Yet then my judgment knew no reason why
My most full flame should afterwards burn clearer.
But reckoning time, whose million'd accidents
Creep in 'twixt vows and change decrees of kings,
Tan sacred beauty, blunt the sharp'st intents,
Divert strong minds to the course of altering things;
Alas, why, fearing of time's tyranny,
Might I not then say 'Now I love you best,'
When I was certain o'er incertainty,
Crowning the present, doubting of the rest?
   Love is a babe; then might I not say so,
   To give full growth to that which still doth grow?

CXVI.

LET me not to the marriage of true minds
Admit impediments. Love is not love
Which alters when it alteration finds,
Or bends with the remover to remove:
O, no! it is an ever-fixèd mark
That looks on tempests and is never shaken:
It is the star to every wandering bark,
Whose worth's unknown, although his height be
  taken.
Love's not Time's fool, though rosy lips and cheeks
Within his bending sickle's compass come;
Love alters not with his brief hours and weeks,
But bears it out even to the edge of doom.
 If this be error and upon me proved,
 I never writ, nor no man ever loved.

CXVII.

Accuse me thus : that I have scanted all
Wherein I should your great deserts repay,
Forgot upon your dearest love to call,
Whereto all bonds do tie me day by day ;
That I have frequent been with unknown minds
And given to time your own dear-purchased right ;
That I have hoisted sail to all the winds
Which should transport me farthest from your sight.
Book both my wilfulness and errors down
And on just proof surmise accumulate ;
Bring me within the level of your frown,
But shoot not at me in your waken'd hate ;
    Since my appeal says I did strive to prove
    The constancy and virtue of your love.

CXVIII.

Like as, to make our appetites more keen,
With eager compounds we our palate urge,
As, to prevent our maladies unseen,
We sicken to shun sickness when we purge,
Even so, being full of your ne'er-coying sweetness,
To bitter sauces did I frame my feeding
And, sick of welfare, found a kind of meetness
To be diseased ere that there was true needing.
Thus policy in love, to anticipate
The ills that were not, grew to faults assured
And brought to medicine a healthful state
Which, rank of goodness, would by ill be cured :
  But thence I learn, and find the lesson true,
  Drugs poison him that so fell sick of you.

CXIX.

WHAT potions have I drunk of Siren tears,
Distill'd from limbecks foul as hell within,
Applying fears to hopes and hopes to fears,
Still losing when I saw myself to win !
What wretched errors hath my heart committed,
Whilst it hath thought itself so blessed never !
How have mine eyes out of their spheres been
  fitted
In the distraction of this madding fever !
O benefit of ill ! now I find true
That better is by evil still made better ;
And ruin'd love, when it is built anew,
Grows fairer than at first, more strong, far greater.
 So I return rebuked to my content
  And gain by ill thrice more than I have spent.

CXX.

THAT you were once unkind befriends me now,
And for that sorrow which I then did feel
Needs must I under my transgression bow,
Unless my nerves were brass or hammer'd steel.
For if you were by my unkindness shaken
As I by yours, you've pass'd a hell of time,
And I, a tyrant, have no leisure taken
To weigh how once I suffer'd in your crime.
O, that our night of woe might have remember'd
My deepest sense, how hard true sorrow hits,
And soon to you, as you to me, then tender'd
The humble salve which wounded bosoms fits !
   But that your trespass now becomes a fee ;
   Mine ransoms yours, and yours must ransom me.

CXXI.

'Tis better to be vile than vile esteem'd,
When not to be receives reproach of being,
And the just pleasure lost which is so deem'd
Not by our feeling but by others' seeing:
For why should others' false adulterate eyes
Give salutation to my sportive blood?
Or on my frailties why are frailer spies,
Which in their wills count bad what I think
    good?
No, I am that I am, and they that level
At my abuses reckon up their own:
I may be straight, though they themselves be
    bevel;
By their rank thoughts my deeds must not be
    shown;
  Unless this general evil they maintain,
  All men are bad, and in their badness reign.

CXXII.

THY gift, thy tables, are within my brain
Full character'd with lasting memory,
Which shall above that idle rank remain
Beyond all date, even to eternity ;
Or at the least, so long as brain and heart
Have faculty by nature to subsist ;
Till each to razed oblivion yield his part
Of thee, thy record never can be miss'd.
That poor retention could not so much hold,
Nor need I tallies thy dear love to score ;
Therefore to give them from me was I bold,
To trust those tables that receive thee more :
    To keep an adjunct to remember thee
    Were to import forgetfulness in me.

CXXIII.

No, Time, thou shalt not boast that I do change :
Thy pyramids built up with newer might
To me are nothing novel, nothing strange ;
They are but dressings of a former sight.
Our dates are brief, and therefore we admire
What thou dost foist upon us that is old,
And rather make them born to our desire
Than think that we before have heard them told.
Thy registers and thee I both defy,
Not wondering at the present nor the past,
For thy records and what we see doth lie,
Made more or less by thy continual haste.
    This I do vow and this shall ever be ;
    I will be true, despite thy scythe and thee.

CXXIV.

If my dear love were but the child of state,
it might for Fortune's bastard be unfather'd,
As subject to Time's love or to Time's hate,
Weeds among weeds, or flowers with flowers gather'd.
No, it was builded far from accident;
It suffers not in smiling pomp, nor falls
Under the blow of thralled discontent,
Whereto the inviting time our fashion calls:
It fears not policy, that heretic,
Which works on leases of short-number'd hours,
But all alone stands hugely politic,
That it nor grows with heat nor drowns with showers.
   To this I witness call the fools of time,
   Which die for goodness, who have lived for crime.

CXXV.

WERE 'T aught to me I bore the canopy,
With my extern the outward honouring,
Or laid great bases for eternity,
Which prove more short than waste or ruining?
Have I not seen dwellers on form and favour
Lose all, and more, by paying too much rent,
For compound sweet forgoing simple savour,
Pitiful thrivers, in their gazing spent?
No, let me be obsequious in thy heart,
And take thou my oblation, poor but free,
Which is not mix'd with seconds, knows no art,
But mutual render, only me for thee.
   Hence, thou suborn'd informer! a true soul
   When most impeach'd stands least in thy control.

ENVOY.

CXXVI.

O, THOU, my lovely boy, who in thy power
Dost hold Time's fickle glass, his sickle, hour;
Who hast by waning grown, and therein show'st
Thy lovers withering as thy sweet self grow'st;
If Nature, sovereign mistress over wrack,
As thou goest onwards, still will pluck thee back,
She keeps thee to this purpose, that her skill
May time disgrace and wretched minutes kill.
Yet fear her, O thou minion of her pleasure!
She may detain, but not still keep, her treasure:
Her audit, though delay'd, answer'd must be,
And her quietus is to render thee.

FINIS.

TO ——

CXXVII. (I.)

In the old age black was not counted fair,
Or if it were, it bore not beauty's name ;
But now is black beauty's successive heir,
And beauty slander'd with a bastard's shame :
For since each hand hath put on Nature's power,
Fairing the foul with art's false borrow'd face,
Sweet beauty hath no name, no holy bower,
But is profaned, if not lives in disgrace.
Therefore my mistress' brows are raven black,
Her eyes so suited, and they mourners seem
At such who, not born fair, no beauty lack,
Slandering creation with a false esteem :
   Yet so they mourn, becoming of their woe,
   That every tongue says beauty should look so.

CXXVIII. (II.)

How oft, when thou, my music, music play'st
Upon that blessed wood whose motion sounds
With thy sweet fingers, when thou gently sway'st
The wiry concord that mine ear confounds,
Do I envy those jacks that nimble leap
To kiss the tender inward of thy hand,
Whilst my poor lips, which should that harvest
     reap,
At the wood's boldness by thee blushing stand!
To be so tickled, they would change their state
And situation with those dancing chips,
O'er whom thy fingers walk with gentle gait,
Making dead wood more blest than living lips.
  Since saucy jacks so happy are in this,
    Give them thy fingers, me thy lips to kiss.

CXXIX. (III.)

THE expense of spirit in a waste of shame
Is lust in action ; and till action, lust
Is perjured, murderous, bloody, full of blame,
Savage, extreme, rude, cruel, not to trust,
Enjoy'd no sooner but despised straight,
Past reason hunted, and no sooner had
Past reason hated, as a swallow'd bait
On purpose laid to make the taker mad ;
Mad in pursuit and in possession so ;
Had, having, and in quest to have, extreme ;
A bliss in proof, and proved, a very woe ;
Before, a joy proposed ; behind, a dream.
    All this the world well knows ; yet none knows well
    To shun the heaven that leads men to this hell.

CXXX. (IV.)

My mistress' eyes are nothing like the sun ;
Coral is far more red than her lip's red ;
If snow be white, why then her breasts are dun ;
If hairs be wires, black wires grow on her head.
I have seen roses damask'd, red and white,
But no such roses see I in her cheeks ;
And in some perfumes is there more delight
Than in the breath that from my mistress reeks.
I love to hear her speak, yet well I know
That music hath a far more pleasing sound ;
I grant I never saw a goddess go ;
My mistress, when she walks, treads on the ground :
   And yet, by heaven, I think my love as rare
   As any she belied with false compare.

CXXXI. (V.)

Thou art as tyrannous, so as thou art,
As those whose beauties proudly make them cruel :
For well thou know'st to my dear doting heart
Thou art the fairest and most precious jewel.
Yet, in good faith, some say that thee behold
Thy face hath not the power to make love groan :
To say they err I dare not be so bold,
Although I swear it to myself alone.
And, to be sure that is not false I swear,
A thousand groans, but thinking on thy face,
One on another's neck, do witness bear
Thy black is fairest in my judgment's place.
    In nothing art thou black save in thy deeds,
    And thence this slander, as I think, proceeds.

CXXXII. (VI.)

THINE eyes I love, and they, as pitying me,
Knowing thy heart torments me with disdain,
Have put on black and loving mourners be,
Looking with pretty ruth upon my pain.
And truly not the morning sun of heaven
Better becomes the grey cheeks of the east,
Nor that full star that ushers in the even
Doth half that glory to the sober west,
As those two mourning eyes become thy face :
O, let it then as well beseem thy heart
To mourn for me, since mourning doth thee grace,
And suit thy pity like in every part.
    Then will I swear beauty herself is black
    And all they foul that thy complexion lack,

CXXXIII. (VII.)

Beshrew that heart that makes my heart to groan
For that deep wound it gives my friend and me !
Is't not enough to torture me alone,
But slave to slavery my sweet'st friend must be !
Me from myself thy cruel eye hath taken,
And my next self thou harder hast engross'd :
Of him, myself, and thee, I am forsaken ;
A torment thrice threefold thus to be cross'd.
Prison my heart in thy steel bosom's ward,
But then my friend's heart let my poor heart bail ;
Whoe'er keeps me, let my heart be his guard ;
Thou canst not then use rigour in my gaol ;
   And yet thou wilt : for I, being pent in thee,
   Perforce am thine, and all that is in me.

CXXXIV. (VIII.)

So, now I have confess'd that he is thine,
And I myself am mortgaged to thy will,
Myself I'll forfeit, so that other mine
Thou wilt restore, to be my comfort still :
But thou wilt not, nor he will not be free,
For thou art covetous and he is kind ;
He learn'd but surety-like to write for me
Under that bond that him as fast doth bind.
The statute of thy beauty thou wilt take,
Thou usurer, that put'st forth all to use,
And sue a friend came debtor for my sake ;
So him I lose through my unkind abuse.
   Him have I lost ; thou hast both him and me :
   He pays the whole, and yet am I not free.

CXXXV. (IX.)

Whoever hath her wish, thou hast thy ' Will,'
And ' Will ' to boot, and ' Will ' in overplus ;
More than enough am I that vex thee still,
To thy sweet will making addition thus.
Wilt thou, whose will is large and spacious,
Not once vouchsafe to hide my will in thine ?
Shall will in others seem right gracious,
And in my will no fair acceptance shine !
The sea, all water, yet receives rain still
And in abundance addeth to his store ;
So thou, being rich in ' Will,' add to thy ' Will '
One will of mine, to make thy large ' Will ' more.
  Let no unkind ' No ' fair beseechers kill ;
  Think all but one, and me in that one ' Will.'

CXXXVI. (X.)

IF thy soul check thee that I come so near,
Swear to thy blind soul that I was thy 'Will,'
And will, thy soul knows, is admitted there ;
Thus far for love my love-suit, sweet, fulfil.
'Will' will fulfil the treasure of thy love,
Ay, fill it full with wills, and my will one.
In things of great receipt with ease we prove
Among a number one is reckon'd none ;
Then in the number let me pass untold,
Though in thy store's account I one must be ;
For nothing hold me, so it please thee hold
That nothing me, a something sweet to thee :
   Make but my name thy love, and love that still ;
   And then thou lov'st me, for my name is 'Will.'

(Vows.) *

DID not the heavenly rhetoric of thine eye,
'Gainst whom the world cannot hold argument,
Persuade my heart to this false perjury?
Vows for thee broke deserve not punishment.
A woman I forswore : but I will prove,
Thou being a goddess, I forswore not thee :
My vow was earthly, thou a heavenly love ;
Thy grace being gain'd cures all disgrace iu me.
Vows are but breath, and breath a vapour is :
Then thou, fair sun, which on my earth dost shine,
Exhalest this vapour-vow : in thee it is :
If broken then, it is no fault of mine :
    If by me broke, what fool is not so wise
    To lose an oath to win a paradise?

CXXXVII. (XI.)

THOU blind fool, Love, what dost thou to mine eyes,
That they behold, and see not what they see?
They know what beauty is, see where it lies,
Yet what the best is take the worst to be.
If eyes corrupt by over-partial looks
Be anchor'd in the bay where all men ride,
Why of eyes' falsehood hast thou forged hooks,
Whereto the judgment of my heart is tied?
Why should my heart think that a several plot
Which my heart kuows the wide world's common
      place?
Or mine eyes seeing this, say this is not,
To put fair truth upon so foul a face?
  In things right true my heart and eyes have erred,
  And to this false plague are they now transferr'd.

CXXXVIII. (XII.)

WHEN my love swears that she is made of truth
I do believe her, though I know she lies,
That she might think me some untutor'd youth,
Unlearned in the world's false subtleties.
Thus vainly thinking that she thinks me young,
Although she knows my days are past the best,
Simply I credit her false-speaking tongue:
On both sides thus is simple truth suppress'd.
But wherefore says she not she is unjust?
And wherefore say not I that I am old?
O, love's best habit is in seeming trust,
And age in love loves not to have years told:
    Therefore I lie with her and she with me,
    And in our faults by lies we flatter'd be.

CXXXIX. (XIII.)

O, CALL not me to justify the wrong
That thy unkindness lays upon my heart:
Wound me not with thine eye but with thy tongue;
Use power with power and slay me not by art.
Tell me thou lov'st elsewhere, but in my sight,
Dear heart, forbear to glance thine eye aside:
What need'st thou wound with cunning when thy
      might
Is more than my o'er-press'd defence can bide?
Let me excuse thee: ah! my love well knows
Her pretty looks have been mine enemies,
And therefore from my face she turns my foes,
That they elsewhere might dart their injuries:
   Yet do not so; but since I am near slain,
   Kill me outright with looks and rid my pain.

(LOVE IN TEARS.)*

So sweet a kiss the golden sun gives not
To those fresh morning drops upon the rose,
As thy eye-beams, when their fresh rays have smote
The night of dew that on my cheeks down flows:
Nor shines the silver moon one half so bright
Through the transparent bosom of the deep,
As doth thy face through tears of mine give light;
Thou shinest in every tear that I do weep:
No drop but as a coach doth carry thee;
So ridest thou triumphing in my woe.
Do but behold the tears that swell in me,
And they thy glory through my grief will show:
    But do not love thyself; then thou wilt keep
    My tears for glasses, and still make me weep.

c·12·c

CXL. (XIV.)

BE wise as thou art cruel ; do not press
My tongue-tied patience with too much disdain ;
Lest sorrow lend me words and words express
The manner of my pity wanting pain.
If I might teach thee wit, better it were,
Though not to love, yet, love, to tell me so ;
As testy sick men, when their deaths be near,
No news but health from their physicians know ;
For if I should despair, I should grow mad,
And in my madness might speak ill of thee :
Now this ill-wresting world is grown so bad,
Mad slanderers by mad ears believed be.
　That I may not be so, nor thou belied,
　Bear thine eyes straight, though thy proud heart
　　go wide.

CXLI. (XV.)

In faith, I do not love thee with mine eyes,
For they in thee a thousand errors note ;
But 'tis my heart that loves what they despise,
Who in despite of view is pleased to dote ;
Nor are mine ears with thy tongue's tune delighted,
Nor tender feeling, to base touches prone,
Nor taste, nor smell, desire to be invited
To any sensual feast with thee alone :
But my five wits nor my five senses can
Dissuade one foolish heart from serving thee,
Who leaves unsway'd the likeness of a man,
Thy proud heart's slave and vassal wretch to be :
   Only my plague thus far I count my gain,
   That she that makes me sin awards me pain.

CXLII. (XVI.)

Love is my sin and thy dear virtue hate,
Hate of my sin, grounded on sinful loving:
O, but with mine compare thou thine own state,
And thou shalt find it merits not reproving;
Or, if it do, not from those lips of thine,
That have profaned their scarlet ornaments
And seal'd false bonds of love as oft as mine,
Robb'd others' beds' revenues of their rents.
Be it lawful I love thee, as thou lovest those
Whom thine eyes woo as mine importune thee:
Root pity in thy heart, that when it grows
Thy pity may deserve to pitied be.
    If thou dost seek to have what thou dost hide,
    By self-example mayst thou be denied !

CXLIII. (XVII.)

Lo ! as a careful housewife runs to catch
One of her feather'd creatures broke away,
Sets down her babe and makes all swift despatch
In pursuit of the thing she would have stay,
Whilst her neglected child holds her in chase,
Cries to catch her whose busy care is bent
To follow that which flies before her face,
Not prizing her poor infant's discontent ;
So runn'st thou after that which flies from thee,
Whilst I thy babe chase thee afar behind ;
But if thou catch thy hope, turn back to me,
And play the mother's part, kiss me, be kind :
   So will I pray that thou may'st have thy ' Will,
   If thou turn back, and my loud crying still.

CXLIV. (XVIII.)

Two loves I have of comfort and despair,
Which like two spirits do suggest me still :
The better angel is a man right fair,
The worser spirit a woman colour'd ill.
To win me soon to hell, my female evil
Tempteth my better angel from my side,
And would corrupt my saint to be a devil,
Wooing his purity with her foul pride.
And whether that my angel be turn'd fiend
Suspect I may, yet not directly tell ;
But being both from me, both to each friend,
I guess one angel in another's hell :
    Yet this shall I ne'er know, but live in doubt,
    Till my bad angel fire my good one out.

CXLV. (XIX.)

Those lips that Love's own hand did make
Breathed forth the sound that said 'I hate'
To me that languish'd for her sake ;
But when she saw my woeful state,
Straight in her heart did mercy come,
Chiding that tongue that ever sweet
Was used in giving gentle doom,
And taught it thus anew to greet ;
'I hate' she alter'd with an end,
That follow'd it as gentle day
Doth follow night, who like a fiend
From heaven to hell is flown away ;
  'I hate' from hate away she threw,
  And saved my life, saying 'not you.'

CXLVI. (XX.)

Poor soul, the centre of my sinful earth,
[Sport of] these rebel powers that thee array,
Why dost thou pine within and suffer dearth,
Painting thy outward walls so costly gay?
Why so large cost, having so short a lease,
Dost thou upon thy fading mansion spend?
Shall worms, inheritors of this excess,
Eat up thy charge? is this thy body's end?
Then, soul, live thou upon thy servant's loss,
And let that pine to aggravate thy store;
Buy terms divine in selling hours of dross;
Within be fed, without be rich no more:
    So shalt thou feed on Death, that feeds on men,
    And Death once dead, there's no more dying then.

CXLVII. (XXI.)

My love is as a fever, longing still
For that which longer nurseth the disease,
Feeding on that which doth preserve the ill,
The uncertain sickly appetite to please.
My reason, the physician to my love,
Angry that his prescriptions are not kept,
Hath left me, and I desperate now approve
Desire is death, which physic did except.
Past cure I am, now reason is past care,
And frantic-mad with evermore unrest ;
My thoughts and my discourse as madmen's are,
At random from the truth vainly express'd ;
  For I have sworn thee fair and thought thee
    bright,
  Who art as black as hell, as dark as night.

CXLVIII. (XXII.)

O, ME, what eyes hath Love put in my head,
Which have no correspondence with true sight !
Or, if they have, where is my judgment fled,
That censures falsely what they see aright ?
If that be fair whereon my false eyes dote,
What means the world to say it is not so !
If it be not, then love doth well denote,
Love's eye is not so true as all men's 'No.'
How can it ? O, how can Love's eye be true,
That is so vexed with watching and with tears !
No marvel then, though I mistake my view :
The sun itself sees not till heaven clears.
    O cunning Love ! with tears thou keepest me
        blind,
    Lest eyes well-seeing thy foul faults should find.

CXLIX. (XXIII.)

CANST thou, O cruel ! say I love thee not,
When I against myself with thee partake ?
Do I not think on thee, when I forgot
Am of myself, all tyrant, for thy sake ?
Who hateth thee that I do call my friend ?
On whom frown'st thou that I do fawn upon ?
Nay, if thou lour'st on me, do I not spend
Revenge upon myself with present moan ?
What merit do I in myself respect,
That is so proud thy service to despise,
When all my best doth worship thy defect,
Commanded by the motion of thine eyes ?
    But, love, hate on, for now I know thy mind :
    Those that can see thou lovest, and I am blind.

CL. (XXIV.)

O, FROM what power hast thou this powerful might
With insufficiency my heart to sway ?
To make me give the lie to my true sight,
And swear that brightness doth not grace the day ?
Whence hast thou this becoming of things ill,
That in the very refuse of thy deeds
There is such strength and warrantise of skill
That, in my mind, thy worst all best exceeds ?
Who taught thee how to make me love thee more
The more I hear and see just cause of hate ?
O, though I love what others do abhor,
With others thou shouldst not abhor my state :
    If thy unworthiness raised love in me,
    More worthy I to be beloved of thee.

CLI. (XXV.)

Love is too young to know what conscience is :
Yet who knows not conscience is born of love ?
Then, gentle cheater, urge not my amiss,
Lest guilty of my faults thy sweet self prove :
For, thou betraying me, I do betray
My nobler part to my gross body's treason ;
My soul doth tell my body that he may
Triumph in love ; flesh stays no farther reason ;
But, rising at thy name, doth point out thee
As his triumphant prize.   Proud of this pride,
He is contented thy poor drudge to be,
To stand in thy affairs, fall by thy side.
  No want of conscience hold it that I call
  Her 'love' for whose dear love I rise and fall.

CLII. (XXVI.)

In loving thee thou know'st I am forsworn,
But thou art twice forsworn, to me love swearing,
In act thy bed-vow broke and new faith torn
In vowing new hate after new love bearing.
But why of two oaths' breach do I accuse thee,
When I break twenty?   I am perjured most;
For all my vows are oaths but to misuse thee
And all my honest faith in thee is lost,
For I have sworn deep oaths of thy deep kindness,
Oaths of thy love, thy truth, thy constancy,
And to enlighten thee, gave eyes to blindness,
Or made them swear against the thing they see;
　For I have sworn thee fair ; more perjured I,
　To swear against the truth so foul a lie !

Finis.

Selections from the Poems.

I.

BE BOLD.

WHAT wax so frozen but dissolves with tempering,
And yields at last to every light impression?
Things out of hope are compass'd oft with venturing,
Chiefly in love, whose leave exceeds commission :
  Affection faints not like a pale-faced coward,
  But then woos best when most his choice is froward.

Venus and Adonis.

II.

THE WARNING OF ADONIS.

'Thou hadst been gone,' quoth she, 'sweet boy, ere
    this,
But that thou told'st me thou wouldst hunt the boar.
O, be advised ! thou know'st not what it is
With javelin's point a churlish swine to gore,
    Whose tushes never sheathed he whetteth still,
    Like to a mortal butcher bent to kill.

'On his bow-back he hath a battle set
Of bristly pikes, that ever threat his foes ;
His eyes, like glow-worms, shine when he doth fret ;
His snout digs sepulchres where'er he goes ;
    Being moved, he strikes whate'er is in his way,
    And whom he strikes his cruel tushes slay.

'His brawny sides, with hairy bristles arm'd,
Are better proof than thy spear's point can enter ;
His short thick neck cannot be easily harm'd ;
Being ireful, on the lion he will venture :
    The thorny brambles and embracing bushes,
    As fearful of him, part, through whom he rushes.

'Alas, he nought esteems that face of thine,
To which Love's eyes pay tributary gazes ;
Nor thy soft hands, sweet lips and crystal eyne,
Whose full perfection all the world amazes ;
    But having thee at vantage,—wondrous dread !—
    Would root these beauties as he roots the mead.

'O, let him keep his loathsome cabin still ;
Beauty hath nought to do with such foul fiends :
Come not within his danger by thy will ;
They that thrive well take counsel of their friends.
    When thou didst name the boar, not to dissemble,
    I fear'd thy fortune, and my joints did tremble.

'Didst thou not mark my face ? was it not white ?
Saw'st thou not signs of fear lurk in mine eye ?
Grew I not faint ? and fell I not downright ?
Within my bosom, whereon thou dost lie,
    My boding heart pants, beats, and takes no rest,
    But, like an earthquake, shakes thee on my breast.

'For where Love reigns, disturbing Jealousy
Doth call himself Affection's sentinel :
Gives false alarms, suggesteth mutiny,
And in a peaceful hour doth cry " Kill, kill ! "
c-13-c

Distempering gentle Love in his desire,
As air and water do abate the fire.

' This sour informer, this bait-breeding spy,
This canker that eats up Love's tender spring,
This carry-tale, dissentious Jealousy,
That sometime true news, sometime false doth bring,
   Knocks at my heart and whispers in mine ear
   That if I love thee, I thy death should fear.

' And more than so, presenteth to mine eye
The picture of an angry-chafing boar,
Under whose sharp fangs on his back doth lie
An image like thyself, all stain'd with gore ;
   Whose blood upon the fresh flowers being shed
   Doth make them droop with grief and hang the
      head.

' What should I do, seeing thee so indeed,
That tremble at the imagination ?
The thought of it doth make my faint heart bleed,
And fear doth teach it divination :
   I prophesy thy death, my living sorrow,
   If thou encounter with the boar to-morrow.

     .   .   .   .   .   .

[*The intervening six stanzas, recounting the hunting of the
hare, will be found under* STRATFORD PICTURES, *No.* II.]

'Lie quietly, and hear a little more ;
Nay, do not struggle, for thou shalt not rise :
To make thee hate the hunting of the boar,
Unlike myself thou hear'st me moralize,
    Applying this to that, and so to so ;
    For love can comment upon every woe.

'Where did I leave ?' 'No matter where ;' quoth he,
'Leave me, and then the story aptly ends :
The night is spent.' 'Why, what of that?' quoth she.
'I am,' quoth he, 'expected of my friends ;
    And now 'tis dark, and going I shall fall.'
    'In night,' quoth she, 'desire sees best of all.

'But if thou fall, O, then imagine this,
The earth, in love with thee, thy footing trips,
And all is but to rob thee of a kiss.
Rich preys make true men thieves ; so do thy lips
    Make modest Dian cloudy and forlorn,
    Lest she should steal a kiss and die forsworn.

'Now of this dark night I perceive the reason :
Cynthia for shame obscures her silver shine,
Till forging Nature be condemn'd of treason,
For stealing moulds from heaven that were divine ;

Wherein she framed thee in high heaven's despite,
To shame the sun by day and her by night.

'And therefore hath she bribed the Destinies
To cross the curious workmanship of nature,
To mingle beauty with infirmities,
And pure perfection with impure defeature,
    Making it subject to the tyranny
    Of mad mischances and much misery.'

Venus and Adonis.

III.

LOVE.

Love comforteth like sunshine after rain,
But Lust's effect is tempest after sun ;
Love's gentle spring doth always fresh remain,
Lust's winter comes ere summer half be done ;
    Love surfeits not, Lust like a glutton dies ;
    Love is all truth, Lust full of forged lies.

Venus and Adonis.

IV.

DEATH OF ADONIS.

*[The preceding four stanzas, ' A Hunting Morn,' will be
found under* STRATFORD PICTURES, *No. V.]*

By this, she hears the hounds are at a bay;
Whereat she starts, like one that spies an adder
Wreathed up in fatal folds just in his way,
The fear whereof doth make him shake and shudder;
   Even so the timorous yelping of the hounds
   Appals her senses and her spirit confounds.

For now she knows it is no gentle chase,
But the blunt boar, rough bear, or lion proud,
Because the cry remaineth in one place,
Where fearfully the dogs exclaim aloud:
   Finding their enemy to be so curst,
   They all strain courtesy who shall cope him first.

This dismal cry rings sadly in her ear,
Through which it enters to surprise her heart;
Who, overcome by doubt and bloodless fear,
With cold-pale weakness numbs each feeling part:
   Like soldiers, when their captain once doth yield,
   They basely fly and dare not stay the field.

Thus stands she in a trembling ecstasy;
Till, cheering up her senses all dismay'd,
She tells them 'tis a causeless fantasy,
And childish error, that they are afraid;
　　Bids them leave quaking, bids them fear no more :—
　　And with that word she spied the hunted boar,

Whose frothy mouth, bepainted all with red,
Like milk and blood being mingled both together,
A second fear through all her sinews spread,
Which madly hurries her she knows not whither:
　　This way she runs, and now she will no further,
　　But back retires to rate the boar for murther.

A thousand spleens bear her a thousand ways;
She treads the path that she untreads again;
Her more than haste is mated with delays,
Like the proceedings of a drunken brain,
　　Full of respects, yet nought at all respecting;
　　In hand with all things, nought at all effecting.

Here kennell'd in a brake she finds a hound,
And asks the weary caitiff for his master,
And there another licking of his wound,
　Gainst venom'd sores the only sovereign plaster;
　　And here she meets another sadly scowling,
　　To whom she speaks, and he replies with howling.

When he hath ceased his ill-resounding noise,
Another flap-mouth'd mourner, black and grim,
Against the welkin volleys out his voice;
Another and another answer him,
    Clapping their proud tails to the ground below,
    Shaking their scratch'd ears, bleeding as they go.

Look, how the world's poor people are amazed
At apparitions, signs and prodigies,
Whereon with fearful eyes they long have gazed,
Infusing them with dreadful prophecies;
    So she at these sad signs draws up her breath
    And sighing it again, exclaims on Death.

'Hard favour'd tyrant, ugly, meagre, lean,
Hateful divorce of love,'—thus chides she Death,—
'Grim-grinning ghost, earth's worm, what dost thou
        mean
To stifle beauty and to steal his breath,
    Who when he lived, his breath and beauty set
    Gloss on the rose, smell to the violet?

'If he be dead.—O no it, cannot be,
Seeing his beauty, thou should'st strike at it :—
O yes, it may; thou hast no eyes to see,
But hatefully at random dost thou hit.

Thy mark is feeble age, but thy false dart
Mistakes that aim and cleaves an infant's heart.

' Hadst thou but bid beware, then he had spoke,
And, hearing him, thy power had lost his power.
The Destinies will curse thee for this stroke;
They bid thee crop a weed, thou pluck'st a flower :
   Love's golden arrow at him should have fied,
   And not Death's ebon dart, to strike him dead.

'Dost thou drink tears, that thou provokest such
      weeping ?
What may a heavy groan advantage thee?
Why hast thou cast into eternal sleeping
Those eyes that taught all other eyes to see?
   Now Nature cares not for thy mortal vigour,
   Since her best work is ruin'd with thy rigour. '

Here overcome, as one full of dispair,
She vail'd her eyelids, who, like sluices, stopt
The crystal tide that from her two cheeks fair
In the sweet channel of her bosom dropt ;
   But through the flood-gates breaks the silver rain.
   And with his strong course opens them again.

O, how her eyes and tears did lend and borrow !
Her eyes seen in the tears, tears in her eye ;

Both crystals, where they view'd each other's sorrow,
Sorrow that friendly sighs sought still to dry ;
   But like a stormy day, now wind, now rain,
   Sighs dry her cheeks, tears make them wet again.

Variable passions throng her constant woe,
As striving who should best become her grief ;
All entertain'd, each passion labours so,
That every present sorrow seemeth chief,
   But none is best : then join they all together,
   Like many clouds consulting for foul weather.

By this, far off she hears some huntsman hollo ;
A nurse's song ne'er pleased her babe so well :
The dire imagination she did follow
The sound of hope doth labour to expel ;
   For now reviving joy bids her rejoice,
   And flatters her it is Adonis' voice.

Whereat her tears began to turn their tide,
Being prison'd in her eye like pearls in glass ;
Yet sometimes falls an orient drop beside,
Which her cheek melts, as scorning it should pass,
   To wash the foul face of the sluttish ground,
   Who is but drunken when she seemeth drown'd.

O hard-believing love, how strange it seems
Not to believe, and yet too credulous !
Thy weal and woe are both of them extremes ;
Despair and hope makes thee ridiculous :
    The one doth flatter thee in thoughts unlikely,
    In likely thoughts the other kills thee quickly.

Now she unweaves the web that she hath wrought ;
Adonis lives, and Death is not to blame ;
It was not she that call'd him all-to naught :
Now she adds honours to his hateful name ;
    She clepes him king of graves and grave for kings,
    Imperious supreme of all mortal things.

'No, no, 'quoth she, 'sweet Death, I did but jest ;
Yet pardon me I felt a kind of fear
When as I met the boar, that bloody beast,
Which knows no pity, but is still severe ;
    Then, gentle shadow,—truth I must confess,—
    I rail'd on thee, fearing my love's decease.

'Tis not my fault : the boar provoked my tongue ;
Be wreak'd on him, invisible commander ;
'Tis he, foul creature, that hath done thee wrong ;
I did but act, he's author of thy slander :

Grief hath two tongues, and never woman yet
Could rule them both without ten women's wit.'

Thus hoping that Adonis is alive,
Her rash suspect she doth extenuate ;
And that his beauty may the better thrive,
With Death she humbly doth insinuate ;
    Tells him of trophies, statues, tombs, and stories
    His victories, his triumphs and his glories.

'O Jove, ' quoth she, 'how much a fool was I
To be of such a weak and silly mind
To wail his death who lives and must not die
Till mutual overthrow of mortal kind !
    For he being dead, with him is beauty slain,
    And, beauty dead, black chaos comes again.

'Fie, fie, fond love, thou art so full of fear
As one with treasure laden, hemm'd with thieves ;
Trifles, unwitnessèd with eye or ear,
Thy coward heart with false bethinking grieves.'
    Even at this word she hears a merry horn,
    Whereat she leaps that was but late forlorn.

As falcon to the lure, away she flies ;
The grass stoops not, she treads on it so light ;

And in her haste unfortunately spies
The foul boar's conquest on her fair delight ;
   Which seen, her eyes, as murder'd with the view,
   Like stars ashamed of day, themselves withdrew ;

Or, as the snail, whose tender horns being hit,
Shrinks backward in his shelly cave with pain,
And there, all smother'd up, in shade doth sit,
Long after fearing to creep forth again ;
   So, at his bloody view, her eyes are fled
   Into the deep dark cabins of her head :

Where they resign their office and their light
To the disposing of her troubled brain ;
Who bids them still consort with ugly night,
And never wound the heart with looks again ;
   Who, like a king perplexed in his throne,
   By their suggestion gives a deadly groan,

Whereat each tributary subject quakes ;
As when the wind, imprison'd in the ground,
Struggling for passage, earth's foundation shakes,
Which with cold terror doth men's minds confound.
   This mutiny each part doth so surprise
   That from their dark beds once more leap her eyes ;

And, being open'd, threw unwilling light
Upon the wide wound that the boar had trench'd
In his soft flank ; whose wonted lily white
With purple tears, that his wound wept, was drenched :
    No flower was nigh, no grass, herb, leaf, or weed,
    But stole his blood and seem'd with him to bleed.

This solemn sympathy poor Venus noteth ;
Over one shoulder doth she hang her head ;
Dumbly she passions, franticly she doteth ;
She thinks he could not die, he is not dead :
    Her voice is stopt, her joints forget to bow ;
    Her eyes are mad that they have wept till now.

Upon his hurt she looks so steadfastly,
That her sight dazzling makes the wound seem three ;
And then she reprehends her mangling eye,
That makes more gashes where no breach should be :
    His face seems twain, each several limb is doubled ;
    For oft the eye mistakes, the brain being troubled.

'My tongue cannot express my grief for one,
And yet, ' quoth she, ' behold two Adons dead !
My sighs are blown away, my salt tears gone,
Mine eyes are turn'd to fire, my heart to lead :

Heavy heart's lead, melt at mine eyes' red fire !
So shall I die by drops of hot desire.

'Alas, poor world, what treasure hast thou lost !
What face remains alive that's worth the viewing ?
Whose tongue is music now ? what canst thou boast
Of things long since, or any thing ensuing ?
   The flowers are sweet, their colours fresh and trim ;
   But true-sweet beauty lived and died with him.

'Bonnet nor veil henceforth no creature wear ?
Nor sun nor wind will ever strive to kiss you :
Having no fair to lose, you need not fear ;
The sun doth scorn you and the wind doth hiss you :
   But when Adonis lived, sun and sharp air
   Lurk'd like two thieves, to rob him of his fair :

'And therefore would he put his bonnet on,
Under whose brim the gaudy sun would peep ;
The wind would blow it off and, being gone,
Play with his locks : then would Adonis weep ;
   And straight, in pity of his tender years,
   They both would strive who first should dry his tears.

'To see his face the lion walk'd along
Behind some hedge, because he would not fear him :

To recreate himself when he hath sung,
The tiger would be tame and gently hear him ;
 If he had spoke, the wolf would leave his prey
 And never fright the silly lamb that day.

' When he beheld his shadow in the brook,
The fishes spread on it their golden gills ;
When he was by, the birds such pleasure took,
That some would sing, some other in their bills
 Would bring him mulberries and ripe-red cherries ;
 He fed them with his sight, they him with berries.

' But this foul, grim, and urchin-snouted boar,
Whose downward eye still looketh for a grave,
Ne'er saw the beauteous livery that he wore ;
Witness the entertainment that he gave :
 If he did see his face, why then I know
 He thought to kiss him, and hath kill'd him so.

''Tis true, 'tis true ; thus was Adonis slain :
He ran upon the boar with his sharp spear,
Who did not whet his teeth at him again,
But by a kiss thought to persuade him there ;
 And nuzzling in his flank, the loving swine
 Sheathed unaware the tusk in his soft groin.

' Had I been tooth'd like him, I must confess,
With kissing him I should have kill'd him first ;
But he is dead, and never did he bless
My youth with his ; the more am I accurst.'
   With this, she falleth in the place she stood,
   And stains her face with his congealed blood.

She looks upon his lips, and they are pale ;
She takes him by the hand, and that is cold ;
She whispers in his ear a heavy tale,
As if they heard the woeful words she told ;
   She lifts the coffer-lids that close his eyes,
   Where, lo, two lamps, burnt out, in darkness lies ;

Two glasses, where herself herself beheld
A thousand times, and now no more reflect ;
Their virtue lost, wherein they late excell'd,
And every beauty robb'd of his effect :
   ' Wonder of time,' quoth she, ' this is my spite,
   That, thou being dead, the day should yet be light.

'Since thou art dead, lo, here I prophesy :
Sorrow on love hereafter shall attend :
It shall be waited on with jealousy,
Find sweet beginning, but unsavoury end.

Ne'er settled equally, but high or low,
That all love's pleasure shall not match his woe.

' It shall be fickle, false and full of fraud,
Bud and be blasted in a breathing-while;
The bottom poison, and the top o'erstraw'd
With sweets that shall the truest sight beguile:
  The strongest body shall it make most weak,
  Strike the wise dumb and teach the fool to speak.

' It shall be sparing and too full of riot,
Teaching decrepit age to tread the measures;
The staring ruffian shall it keep in quiet,
Pluck down the rich, enrich the poor with treasures;
  It shall be raging-mad and silly-mild,
  Make the young old, the old become a child.

' It shall suspect where is no cause of fear,
It shall not fear where it should most mistrust;
It shall be merciful and too severe,
And most deceiving when it seems most just;
  Perverse it shall be where it shows most toward,
  Put fear to valour, courage to the coward.

' It shall be cause of war and dire events,
And set dissension 'twixt the son and sire;

Subject and servile to all discontents,
As dry combustious matter is to fire:
 Sith in his prime Death doth my love destroy,
 They that love best their loves shall not enjoy.'

By this, the boy that by her side lay kill'd
Was melted like a vapour from her sight,
And in his blood that on the ground lay spill'd,
A purple flower sprung up, chequer'd with white,
 Resembling well his pale cheeks and the blood
 Which in round drops upon their whiteness stood.

She bows her head, the new sprung flower to smell,
Comparing it to her Adonis' breath,
And says, within her bosom it shall dwell,
Since he himself is reft from her by death :
 She crops the stalk, and in the breach appears
 Green dropping sap, which she compares to tears.

' Poor flower,' quoth she, ' this was thy father's guise—
Sweet issue of a more sweet-smelling sire—
For every little grief to wet his eyes :
To grow unto himself was his desire,
 And so 'tis thine ; but know, it is as good
 To wither in my breast as in his blood.

'Here was thy father's bed, here in my breast ;
Thou art the next of blood, and 'tis thy right :
Lo, in this hollow cradle take thy rest,
My throbbing heart shall rock thee day and night :
   There shall not be one minute in an hour
   Wherein I will not kiss my sweet love's flower.'

Thus weary of the world, away she hies,
And yokes her silver doves ; by whose swift aid
Their mistress mounted through the empty skies
In her light chariot quickly is convey'd ;
   Holding their course to Paphos, where their queen
   Means to immure herself and not be seen.

Venus and Adonis.

STRATFORD PICTURES.

(1.)

THE STALLION.

But lo, from forth a copse that neighbours by,
A breeding jennet, lusty, young and proud,
Adonis' trampling courser doth espy,
And forth she rushes, snorts and neighs aloud :
   The strong-neck'd steed, being tied unto a tree,
   Breaketh his rein, and to her straight goes he.

Imperiously he leaps, he neighs, he bounds,
And now his woven girths he breaks asunder;
The bearing earth with his hard hoof he wounds,
Whose hollow womb resounds like heaven's thunder;
   The iron bit he crusheth 'tween his teeth,
   Controlling what he was controlled with.

His ears up-prick'd; his braided hanging mane
Upon his compass'd crest now stand on end;
His nostrils drink the air, and forth again,
As from a furnace, vapours doth he send:
   His eye, which scornfully glisters like fire,
   Shows his hot courage and his high desire.

Sometime he trots, as if he told the steps,
With gentle majesty and modest pride;
Anon he rears upright, curvets and leaps,
As who should say 'Lo, thus my strength is tried,
   And this I do to captivate the eye
   Of the fair breeder that is standing by.'

What recketh he his rider's angry stir,
His flattering 'Holla,' or his 'Stand, I say'?
What cares he now for curb or pricking spur?
For rich caparisons or trapping gay?

He sees his love, and nothing else he sees,
For nothing else with his proud sight agrees.

Look, when a painter would surpass the life,
In limning out a well-proportioned steed,
His art with nature's workmanship at strife,
As if the dead the living should exceed ;
  So did this horse excel a common one
  In shape, in courage, colour, pace and bone.

Round-hoof'd, short-jointed, fetlocks shag and long,
Broad breast, full eye, small head and nostril wide,
High crest, short ears, straight legs and passing strong,
Thin mane, thick tail, broad buttock, tender hide :
  Look, what a horse should have he did not lack,
  Save a proud rider on so proud a back.

Sometime he scuds far off and there he stares ;
Anon he starts at stirring of a feather ;
To bid the wind a base he now prepares,
And whether he run or fly they know not whether ;
  For through his mane and tail the high wind sings,
  Fanning the hairs, who wave like feather'd wings.

Venus and Adonis.

STRATFORD PICTURES. (2.)

WIND AND RAIN.

LIKE a red morn, that ever yet betoken'd
   Wreck to the seaman, tempest to the field,
Sorrow to shepherds, woe unto the birds,
Gusts and foul flaws to herdmen and to herds.

Even as the wind is hush'd before it raineth.

Venus and Adonis.

STRATFORD PICTURES. (3.)

THE EDGE O' DARK.

LOOK, the world's comforter, with weary gait,
  His day's hot task hath ended in the west;
The owl, night's herald, shrieks, 'tis very late;
  The sheep are gone to fold, birds to their nest;
And coal-black clouds that shadow heaven's light
Do summon us to part and bid good-night.

Venus and Adonis.

STRATFORD PICTURES. (4.)

THE HUNTED HARE.

'BUT if thou needs wilt hunt, be ruled by me;
Uncouple at the timorous flying hare,
Or at the fox which lives by subtlety,
Or at the roe which no encounter dare :
   Pursue these fearful creatures o'er the downs,
   And on thy well-breathed horse keep with thy
      hounds.

'And when thou hast on foot the purblind hare,
Mark the poor wretch, to overshoot his troubles
How he outruns the wind and with what care
He cranks and crosses with a thousand doubles :
   The many musets through the which he goes
   Are like a labyrinth to amaze his foes.

'Sometime he runs among a flock of sheep,
To make the cunning hounds mistake their smell,
And sometime where earth-delving conies keep,
To stop the loud pursuers in their yell,
   And sometime sorteth with a herd of deer :
   Danger deviseth shifts ; wit waits on fear :

' For there his smell with others being mingled,
The hot scent-snuffing hounds are driven to doubt,
Ceasing their clamorous cry till they have singled
With much ado the cold fault cleanly out ;
    Then do they spend their mouths : Echo replies,
    As if another chase were in the skies.

' By this, poor Wat, far off upon a hill,
Stands on his hinder legs with listening ear,
To hearken if his foes pursue him still :
Anon their loud alarums he doth hear ;
    And now his grief may be compared well
    To one sore sick that hears the passing-bell.

'Then shalt thou see the dew-bedabbled wretch
Turn, and return, indenting with the way ;
Each envious brier his weary legs doth scratch,
Each shadow makes him stop, each murmur stay :
    For misery is trodden on by many,
    And being low never relieved by any.
                              Venus and Adonis.

STRATFORD PICTURES. (5.)

A Hunting Morn.

'Lo, here the gentle lark, weary of rest,
From his moist cabinet mounts up on high,
And wakes the morning, from whose silver breast
The sun ariseth in his majesty;
　　Who doth the world so gloriously behold
　　That cedar-tops and hills seem burnish'd gold.

Venus salutes him with this fair good-morrow:
'O thou clear god, and patron of all light,
From whom each lamp and shining star doth borrow
The beauteous influence that makes him bright,
　　There lives a son that suck'd an earthly mother,
　　May lend thee light, as thou dost lend to other.'

This said, she hasteth to a myrtle grove,
Musing the morning is so much o'erworn,
And yet she hears no tidings of her love:
She harkens for his hounds and for his horn:
　　Anon she hears them chant it lustily,
　　And all in haste she coasteth to the cry.

And as she runs, the bushes in the way
Some catch her by the neck, some kiss her face,

Some twine about her thigh to make her stay :
She wildly breaketh from their strict embrace,
  Like a milch doe, whose swelling dugs do ache,
  Hasting to feed her fawn hid in some brake.

Venus and Adonis.

STRATFORD PICTURES. (6.)

The Brook-side.

Soarce had the sun dried up the dewy morn,
  And scarce the herd gone to the hedge for shade,
When Cytherea, all in love forlorn,
  A longing tarriance for Adonis made
    Under an osier
    Growing by a brook.

The Passionate Pilgrim.

IV.

LUCRECE ASLEEP.

Without the bed her other fair hand was,
On the green coverlet ; whose perfect white
Show'd like an April daisy on the grass,

With pearly sweat, resembling dew of night.
Her eyes, like marigolds, had sheathed their light,
  And canopied in darkness sweetly lay,
  Till they might open to adorn the day.

Her hair, like golden threads, play'd with her breath ;
O modest wantons ! wanton modesty !
Showing life's triumph in the map of death,
And death's dim look in life's mortality ;
Each in her sleep themselves so beautify,
  As if between them twain there was no strife,
  But that life lived in death, and death in life.

Rape of Lucrece.

v.

VAIN PROFIT.

THOSE that much covet are with gain so fond,
For what they have not, that which they possess
They scatter and unloose it from their bond,
And so, by hoping more, the profit of excess
  Is but to surfeit, and such griefs sustain,
  That they prove bankrupt in this poor-rich gain.

The aim of all is but to nurse the life
With honour, wealth, and ease, in waning age ;
And in this arm there is such thwarting strife,
That one for all, or all for one we gage ;
As life for honour in fell battle's rage ;
    Honour for wealth ; and oft that wealth doth cost
    The death of all, and all together lost.

So that in venturing ill we leave to be
The things we are for that which we expect ;
And this ambitious foul infirmity,
In having much, torments us with defect
Of that we have : so then we do neglect
    The thing we have ; and, all for want of wit,
    Make something nothing by augmenting it.
                        Rape of Lucrece.

VI.

OPPORTUNITY.

THE aged man that coffers-up his gold
Is plagued with cramps and gouts and painful fits ;
And scarce hath eyes his treasure to behold,
But like still-pining Tantalus he sits,
And useless barns the harvest of his wits ;

Having no other pleasure of his gain
But torment that it cannot cure his pain.

So then he hath if when he cannot use it,
And leaves it to be master'd by his young ;
Who in their pride do presently abuse it :
Their father was too weak, and they too strong,
To hold their cursed-blessed fortune long.
   The sweets we wish for turn to loathed sours
   Even in the moment that we call them ours.

Unruly blasts wait on the tender spring ;
Unwholesome weeds take root with precious flowers ;
The adder hisses where the sweet birds sing ;
What virtue breeds iniquity devours :
We have no good that we can say is ours,
   But ill-annex'd Opportunity
   Or kills his life or else his quality.

O, Opportunity, thy guilt is great !
'Tis thou that executest the traitor's treason :
Thou set'st the wolf where he the lamb may get ;
Whoever plots the sin, thou 'point'st the season ;
'Tis thou that spurn'st at right, at law, at reason ;
   And in thy shady cell, where none may spy him,
   Sits Sin, to seize the souls that wander by him.

' Thou makest the vestal violate her oath ;
Thou blow'st the fire when temperance is thaw'd ;
Thou smother'st honesty, thou murder'st troth ;
Thou foul abettor ! thou notorious bawd !
Thou plantest scandal and displacest laud :
    Thou ravisher, thou traitor, thou false thief,
    Thy honey turns to gall, thy joy to grief !

' Thy secret pleasure turns to open shame,
Thy private feasting to a public fast,
Thy smoothing titles to a ragged name,
Thy sugar'd tongue to bitter wormwood taste :
Thy violent vanities can never last.
    How comes it then, vile Opportunity,
    Being so bad, such numbers seek for thee ?

' When wilt thou be the humble suppliant's friend,
And bring him where his suit may be obtain'd ? '
When wilt thou short an hour great strifes to end ?
Or free that soul which wretchedness hath chain'd ?
Give physic to the sick, ease to the pain'd ?
    The poor, lame, blind, halt, creep, cry out for thee ;
    But they ne'er meet with Opportunity.

' The patient dies while the physician sleeps ;
The orphan pines while the oppressor feeds ;

Justice is feasting while the widow weeps ;
Advice is sporting while infection breeds :
Thou grant'st no time for charitable deeds :
   Wrath, envy, treason, rape, and murder's rages,
   Thy heinous hours wait on them as their pages.

Rape of Lucrece.

VII.

TIME.

Thou ceaseless lackey to eternity.

Time's glory is to calm contending kings,
To unmask falsehood and bring truth to light,
To stamp the seal of time in aged things,
To wake the morn and sentinel the night,
To wrong the wronger till he render right,
   To ruinate proud buildings with thy hours,
   And smear with dust their glittering golden towers ;

To fill with worm-holes stately monuments,
To feed oblivion with decay of things,
To blot old books and alter their contents,
To pluck the quills from ancient ravens' wings,
To dry the old oak's sap and cherish springs,
   To spoil antiquities of hammer'd steel,
   And turn the giddy round of Fortune's wheel ;

To show the beldam daughters of her daughter,
To make the child a man, the man a child,
To slay the tiger that doth live by slaughter,
To tame the unicorn and lion wild,
To mock the subtle in themselves beguiled,
   To cheer the ploughman with increaseful crops,
   And waste huge stones with little water-drops.

Why work'st thou mischief in thy pilgrimage,
Unless thou couldst return to make amends?
One poor retiring minute in an age
Would purchase thee a thousand thousand friends,
Lending him wit that to bad debtors lends:
   (O, this dread night, wouldst thou one hour come
      back,
   I could prevent this storm and shun thy wrack!)

                    Rape of Lucrece.

VIII.

WORDS.

Out, idle words, servants to shallow fools!
Unprofitable sounds, weak arbitrators!
Busy yourselves in skill-contending schools:

Debate where leisure serves with dull debaters;
To trembling clients be you mediators:
  For me, I force not argument a straw,
  Since that my case is past the help of law.

Rape of Lucrece.

IX.

TRUE GRIEF.

Thus cavils she with every thing she sees:
True grief is fond and testy as a child,
Who wayward once, his mood with nought agrees:
Old woes, not infant sorrows, bear them mild;
Continuance tames the one; the other wild,
  Like an unpractised swimmer plunging still,
  With too much labour drowns for want of skill.

So she, deep-drenched in a sea of care,
Holds disputation with each thing she views,
And to herself all sorrow doth compare;
No object but her passion's strength renews;
And as one shifts, another straight ensues:
  Sometime her grief is dumb and hath no words;
  Sometime 'tis mad and too much talk affords.

c-15-c

The little birds that tune their morning's joy,
Make her moans mad with their sweet melody:
For mirth doth search the bottom of annoy ;
Sad souls are slain in merry company ;
Grief best is pleased with grief's society :
　　True sorrow then is feelingly sufficed
　　When with like semblance it is sympathized.

'Tis double death to drown in ken of shore ;
He ten times pines that pines beholding food ;
To see the salve doth make the wound ache more ;
Great grief grieves most at that would do it good ;
Deep woes roll forward like a gentle flood,
　　Who, being stopp'd, the bounding banks o'erflows ;
　　Grief dallied with nor law nor limit knows.

Rape of Lucrece.

X.

MEN AND WOMEN.

For men have marble, women waxen, minds,
And therefore are they form'd as marble will ;
The weak oppress'd, the impression of strange kinds
Is form'd in them by force, by fraud, or skill :
Then call them not the authors of their ill,

No more than wax shall be accounted evil
Wherein is stamp'd the semblance of a devil.

Their smoothness, like a goodly champaign plain,
Lays open all the little worms that creep ;
In men, as in a rough-grown grove, remain
Cave-keeping evils that obscurely sleep :
Through crystal walls each little mote will peep :
   Though men can cover crimes with bold stern
      looks,
   Poor women's faces are their own faults' books.

No man inveigh against the wither'd flower,
But chide rough weather that the flower hath kill'd ;
Not that devour'd, but that which doth devour,
Is worthy blame.   O, let it not be hild
Poor women's faults, that they are so fulfill'd
   With men's abuses : those proud lords, to blame,
   Make weak-made women tenants to their shame.
Rape of Lucrece.

XI.

LUCRECE AND THE PICTURE OF TROY.

   But long she thinks till he return again,
   And yet the duteous vassal scarce is gone.

The weary time she cannot entertain,
For now 'tis stale to sigh, to weep, and groan :
So woe hath wearied woe, moan tired moan,
    That she her plaints a little while doth stay,
    Pausing for means to mourn some newer way.

At last she calls to mind where hangs a piece
Of skilful painting, made for Priam's Troy :
Before the which is drawn the power of Greece,
For Helen's rape the city to destroy,
Threatening cloud-kissing Ilion with annoy ;
    Which the conceited painter drew so proud,
    As heaven, it seem'd, to kiss the turrets bow'd.

A thousand lamentable objects there,
In scorn of nature, art gave lifeless life ;
Many a dry drop seemed a weeping tear,
Shed for the slaughter'd husband by the wife :
The red blood reek'd, to show the painter's strife ;
    And dying eyes gleam'd forth their ashy lights,
    Like dying coals burnt out in tedious nights.

There might you see the labouring pioneer
Begrimed with sweat, and smeared all with dust :
And from the towers of Troy there would appear

The very eyes of men through loop-holes thrust,
Gazing upon the Greeks with little lust :
   Such sweet observance in this work was had,
   That one might see those far-off eyes look sad.

In great commanders grace and majesty
You might behold, triumphing in their faces ;
In youth, quick bearing and dexterity ;
And here and there the painter interlaces
Pale cowards, marching on with trembling paces ;
   Which heartless peasants did so well resemble,
   That one would swear he saw them quake and
      tremble.

In Ajax and Ulysses, O, what art
Of physiognomy might one behold !
The face of either cipher'd either's heart ;
Their face their manners most expressly told :
In Ajax' eyes blunt rage and rigour roll'd ;
   But the mild glance that sly Ulysses lent
   Show'd deep regard and smiling government.

There pleading might you see great Nestor stand,
As 'twere encouraging the Greeks to fight ;
Making such sober action with his hand,

That it beguiled attention, charm'd the sight :
In speech, it seem'd, his beard, all silver white,
  Wagg'd up and down, and from his lips did fly
  Thin winding breath, which purl'd up to the sky.

About him were a press of gaping faces,
Which seem'd to swallow up his sound advice ;
All jointly listening, but with several graces,
As if some mermaid did their ears entice,
Some high, some low, the painter was so nice ;
  The scalps of many, almost hid behind,
  To jump up higher seem'd, to mock the mind.

Here one man's hand lean'd on another's head,
His nose being shadow'd by his neighbour's ear ;
Here one being throng'd bears back, all boll'n and
    red ;
Another smother'd seems to pelt and swear ;
And in their rage such signs of rage they bear,
  As, but for loss of Nestor's golden words,
  It seem'd they would debate with angry swords.

For much imaginary work was there ;
Conceit deceitful, so compact, so kind,
That for Achilles' image stood his spear,

Griped in an armed hand ; himself, behind,
Was left unseen, save to the eye of mind :
　A hand, a foot, a face, a leg, a head,
　Stood for the whole to be imagined.

And from the walls of strong-besieged Troy
When their brave hope, bold Hector, march'd to field,
Stood many Trojan mothers, sharing joy
To see their youthful sons bright weapons wield ;
And to their hope they such odd action yield,
　That through their light joy seemèd to appear,
　Like bright things stain'd, a kind of heavy fear.

And from the strand of Dardan, where they fought,
To Simois' reedy banks the red blood ran,
Whose waves to imitate the battle sought
With swelling ridges ; and their ranks began
To break upon the galled shore, and then
　Retire again, till, meeting greater ranks,
　They join and shoot their foam at Simois' banks.

To this well-painted piece is Lucrece come,
To find a face where all distress is stell'd.
Many she sees where cares have carved some,
But none where all distress and dolour dwell'd,
Till she despairing Hecuba beheld,

Staring on Priam's wounds with her old eyes,
Which bleeding under Pyrrhus' proud foot lies.

In her the painter had anatomized
Time's ruin, beauty's wreck, and grim care's reign :
Her cheeks with chaps and wrinkles were disguised ;
Of what she was no semblance did remain :
Her blue blood changed to black in every vein,
  Wanting the spring that those shrunk pipes had
    fed,
  Show'd life imprison'd in a body dead.

Rape of Lucrece.

XII.

A LOVER'S COMPLAINT.

FROM off a hill whose concave womb re-worded
A plaintful story from a sistering vale,
My spirits to attend this double voice accorded,
And down I laid to list the sad-tuned tale ;
Ere long espied a fickle maid full pale,
Tearing of papers, breaking rings a-twain,
Storming her world with sorrow's wind and rain.

Upon her head a platted hive of straw,
Which fortified her visage from the sun,
Whereon the thought might think sometime it saw
The carcass of a beauty spent and done :
Time had not scythèd all that youth begun,
Nor youth all quit ; but, spite of heaven's fell rage,
Some beauty peep'd through lattice of sear'd age.

Oft did she heave her napkin to her eyne,
Which on it had conceited characters,
Laundering the silken figures in the brine
That season'd woe had pelleted in tears,
And often reading what contents it bears ;
As often shrieking undistinguish'd woe,
In clamours of all size, both high and low.

Sometimes her levell'd eyes their carriage ride,
As they did battery to the spheres intend ;
Sometime diverted their poor balls are tied
To the orbed earth ; sometimes they do extend
Their view right on ; anon their gazes lend
To every place at once, and, nowhere fix'd,
The mind and sight distractedly commix'd.

Her hair, nor loose nor tied in formal plat,
Proclaim'd in her a careless hand of pride

For some, untuck'd, descended her sheaved hat,
Hanging her pale and pined cheek beside;
Some in her threaden fillet still did bide,
And true to bondage would not break from thence,
Though slackly braided in loose negligence.

A thousand favours from a maund she drew
Of amber, crystal, and of beaded jet,
Which one by one she in a river threw,
Upon whose weeping margent she was set;
Like usury, applying wet to wet,
Or monarch's hands that let not bounty fall
Where want cries some, but where excess begs all.

Of folded schedules had she many a one,
Which she perused, sigh'd, tore, and gave the flood;
Crack'd many a ring of posied gold and bone,
Bidding them find their sepulchres in mud;
Found yet moe letters sadly penn'd in blood,
With sleided silk feat and affectedly
Enswathed, and seal'd to curious secrecy.

These often bathed she in her fluxive eyes,
And often kiss'd, and often 'gan to tear:
Cried, 'O false blood, thou register of lies,
What unapproved witness dost thou bear!
Ink would have seem'd more black and damned here!'

This said, in top of rage the lines she rents,
Big discontent so breaking their contents.

A reverend man that grazed his cattle nigh—
Sometime a blusterer, that the ruffle kuew
Of court, of city, and had let go by
The swiftest hours, observed as they flew—
Towards this afflicted fancy fastly drew,
And, privileged by age, desires to kuow
In brief the grounds and motives of her woe.

So slides he down upon his grained bat,
And comely-distant sits he by her side ;
When he again desires her, being sat,
Her grievance with his hearing to divide :
If that from him there may be aught applied
Which may her suff'ring ecstasy assuage,
'Tis promisc'd in the charity of age.

' Father,' she says, ' though in me you behold
The injury of many a blasting hour,
Let it not tell your judgment I am old ;
Not age, but sorrow, over me hath power :
I might as yet have been a spreading flower,
Fresh to myself, if I had self-applied
Love to myself and to no love beside.

'But, woe is me! too early I attended
A youthful suit—it was to gain my grace—
Of one by nature's outwards so commended,
That maidens' eyes stuck over all his face:
Love lack'd a dwelling, and made him her place;
And when in his fair parts she did abide,
She was new lodged and newly deified.

'His browny locks did hang in crooked curls;
And every light occasion of the wind
Upon his lips their silken parcels hurls.
What's sweet to do, to do will aptly find:
Each eye that saw him did enchant the mind,
For on his visage was in little drawn
What largeness thinks in Paradise was sawn.

'Small show of man was yet upon his chin;
His phœnix down began but to appear
Like unshorn velvet on that termless skin
Whose bare out-bragg'd the web it seem'd to wear:
Yet show'd his visage by that cost more dear;
And nice affections wavering stood in doubt
If best were as it was, or best without.

'His qualities were beauteous as his form,
For maiden-tongued he was, and thereof free;

Yet, if men moved him, was he such a storm
As oft 'twixt May and April is to see,
When winds breathe sweet, unruly though they be.
His rudeness so with his authorized youth
Did livery falseness in a pride of truth.

'Well could he ride, and often men would say,
"That horse his mettle from his rider takes:
Proud of subjection, noble by the sway,
What rounds, what bounds, what course, what stop he
      makes!"
And controversy hence a question takes,
Whether the horse by him became his deed,
Or he his manage by the well-doing steed.

'But quickly on this side the verdict went:
His real habitude gave life and grace
To appertainings and to ornament,
Accomplish'd in himself, not in his case:
All aids, themselves made fairer by their place,
Came for additions; yet their purposed trim
Pieced not his grace, but were all graced by him.

'So on the tip of his subduing tongue
All kind of arguments and question deep,

All replication prompt, and reason strong,
For his advantage still did wake and sleep :
To make the weeper laugh, the laugher weep,
He had the dialect and different skill,
Catching all passions in his craft of will :

' That he did in the general bosom reign
Of young, of old ; and sexes both enchanted,
To dwell with him in thoughts, or to remain
In personal duty, following where he haunted :
Consents bewitch'd, ere he desire, have granted ;
And dialogued for him what he would say,
Ask'd their own wills, and made their wills obey.

' Many there were that did his picture get,
To serve their eyes, and in it put their mind ;
Like fools that in th' imagination set
The goodly objects which abroad they find
Of lands and mansions, theirs in thought assign'd ;
And labouring in moe pleasures to bestow them
Than the true gouty landlord which doth owe them :

' So many have, that never touch'd his hand,
Sweetly supposed them mistress of his heart.
My woeful self, that did in freedom stand,
And was my own fee-simple, not in part,

What with his art in youth, and youth in art,
Threw my affections in his charmed power,
Reserved the stalk and gave him all my flower.

'Yet did I not, as some my equals did,
Demand of him, nor being desired yielded:
Finding myself in honour so forbid,
With safest distance I mine honour shielded:
Experience for me many bulwarks builded
Of proofs new-bleeding, which remain'd the foil
Of this false jewel, and his amorous spoil.

'But, ah, who ever shunn'd by precedent
The destined ill she must herself assay?
Or forced examples, 'gainst her own content,
To put the by-past perils in her way?
Counsel may stop awhile what will not stay;
For when we rage, advice is often seen
By blunting us to make our wits more keen.

'Nor gives it satisfaction to our blood,
That we must curb it upon others' proof;
To be forbod the sweets that seem so good,
For fear of harms that preach in our behoof.
O appetite, from judgment stand aloof!

The one a palate hath that needs will taste,
Though Reason weep, and cry " It is thy last."

' For further I could say " This man's untrue,"
And knew the patterns of his foul beguiling ;
Heard where his plants in others' orchards grew,
Saw how deceits were gilded in his smiling ;
Knew vows were ever brokers to defiling ;
Thought characters and words merely but art,
And bastards of his foul adulterate heart.

' And long upon these terms I held my city,
Till thus he gan besiege me : " Gentle maid,
Have of my suffering youth some feeling pity,
And be not of my holy vows afraid :
That's to ye sworn to none was ever said ;
For feasts of love I have been call'd unto,
Till now did ne'er invite, nor never woo.

' " All my offences that abroad you see
Are errors of the blood, none of the mind ;
Love made them not : with acture they may be,
Where neither party is nor true nor kind :
They sought their shame that so their shame did find ;
And so much less of shame in me remains,
By how much of me their reproach contains.

' " Among the many that mine eyes have seen,
Not one whose flame my heart so much as warm'd,
Or my affection put to the smallest teen,
Or any of my leisures ever charm'd :
Harm have I done to them, but ne'er was harm'd ;
Kept hearts in liveries, but mine own was free,
And reign'd, commanding in his monarchy.

' " Look here, what tributes wounded fancies sent me
Of paled pearls and rubies red as blood ;
Figuring that they their passions likewise lent me
Of grief and blushes, aptly understood
In bloodless white and the encrimson'd mood ;
Effects of terror and dear modesty,
Encamp'd in hearts, but fighting outwardly.

' " And, lo, behold these talents of their hair,
With twisted metal amorously impleach'd,
I have received from many a several fair,
Their kind acceptance weepingly beseech'd,
With the annexions of fair gems enrich'd,
And deep-brain'd sonnets that did amplify
Each stone's dear nature, worth, and quality.

' " The diamond,—why, 'twas beautiful and hard,
Whereto his invised properties did tend ;

c-16-c

The deep-green emerald, in whose fresh regard
Weak sights their sickly radiance do amend ;
The heaven-hued sapphire and the opal blend
With objects manifold : each several stone,
With wit well blazon'd, smiled or made some moan.

' "Lo, all these trophies of affections hot,
Of pensived and subdued desires the tender,
Nature hath charged me that I hoard them not,
But yield them up where I myself must render,
That is, to you, my origin and ender ;
For these, of force, must your oblations be,
Since I their altar, you enpatron me.

' "O, then, advance of yours that phraseless hand,
Whose white weighs down the airy scale of praise ;
Take all these similes to your own command,
Hallow'd with sighs that burning lungs did raise ;
What me your minister, for you obeys,
Works under you ; and to your audit comes
Their distract parcels in combined sums.

' " Lo, this device was sent me from a nun,
Or sister sanctified, of holiest note ;
Which late her noble suit in court did shun,
Whose rarest havings made the blossoms dote ;

For she was sought by spirits of richest coat,
But kept cold distance, and did thence remove,
To spend her living in eternal love.

' " But, O my sweet, what labour is't to leave
The thing we have not, mastering what not strives,
Playing the place which did no form receive,
Playing patient sports in unconstrained gyves ?
She that her fame so to herself contrives,
The scars of battle 'scapeth by the flight,
And makes her absence valiant, not her might.

' " O, pardon me, in that my boast is true :
The accident which brought me to her eye
Upon the moment did her force subdue,
And now she would the caged cloister fly :
Religious love put out Religion's eye :
Not to be tempted, would she be immured,
And now, to tempt, all liberty procured.

' " How mighty then you are, O, hear me tell !
The broken bosoms that to me belong
Have emptied all their fountains in my well,
And mine I pour your ocean all among :
I strong o'er them, and you o'er me being strong,
Must for your victory us all congest,
As compound love to physic your cold breast.

' " My parts had power to charm a sacred nun,
Who, disciplined, ay, dieted in grace,
Believed her eyes when they to assail begun,
All vows and consecrations giving place :
O most potential love ! vow, bond, nor space,
In thee hath neither sting, knot, nor confine,
For thou art all, and all things else are thine.

' " When thou impressest, what are precepts worth
Of stale example ?   When thou wilt inflame,
How coldly those impediments stand forth
Of wealth, of filial fear, law, kindred, fame !
Love's arms are peace, 'gainst rule, 'gainst sense,
        'gainst shame,
And sweetens, in the suffering pangs it bears,
The aloes of all forces, shocks, and fears.

' " Now all these hearts that do on mine depend,
Feeling it break, with bleeding groans they pine ;
And supplicant their sighs to you extend,
To leave the battery that you make 'gainst mine,
Lending soft audience to my sweet design,
And credent soul to that strong-bonded oath
That shall prefer and undertake my troth."

' This said, his watery eyes he did dismount,
Whose sights till then were levell'd on my face ;

Each cheek a river running from a fount
With brinish current downward flowed apace :
O, how the channel to the stream gave grace !
Who glazed with crystal gate the glowing roses
That flame through water which their hue encloses.

'O father, what a hell of witchcraft lies
In the small orb of one particular tear !
But with the inundation of the eyes
What rocky heart to water will not wear ?
What breast so cold that is not warmed here ?
O cleft effect ! cold modesty, hot wrath,
Both fire from hence and chill extincture hath.

'For, lo, his passion, but an art of craft,
Even there resolved my reason into tears ;
There my white stole of chastity I daff'd,
Shook off my sober guards and civil fears ;
Appear to him, as he to me appears,
All melting ; though our drops this difference bore,
His poison'd me, and mine did him restore.

'In him a plenitude of subtle matter,
Applied to cautels, all strange forms receives,
Of burning blushes, or of weeping water,

Or swooning paleness ; and he takes and leaves,
In either's aptness, as it best deceives,
To blush at speeches rank, to weep at woes,
Or to turn white and swoon at tragic shows :

'That not a heart which in his level came
Could 'scape the hail of his all-hurting aim,
Showing fair nature is both kind and tame ;
And, veil'd in them, did win whom he would maim :
Against the thing he sought he would exclaim ;
When he most burn'd in heart-wish'd luxury,
He preach'd pure maid, and praised cold chastity.

'Thus merely with the garment of a Grace
The naked and concealed fiend he cover'd ;
That th' unexperient gave the tempter place,
Which like a cherubin above them hover'd.
Who, young and simple, would not be so lover'd ?
Ay me ! I fell ; and yet do question make
What I should do again for such a sake.

'O, that infected moisture of his eye,
O, that false fire which in his cheeks so glow'd,
O, that forced thunder from his heart did fly,
O, that sad breath his spongy lungs bestow'd,
O, all that borrow'd motion seeming owed,

Would yet again betray the fore-betray'd,
And new pervert a reconciled maid !'

XIII.

LOVE'S FIRE.

(I.)

Cupid laid by his brand, and fell asleep :
A maid of Dian's this advantage found,
And his love-kindling fire did quickly steep
In a cold valley-fountain of that ground ;
Which borrow'd from this holy fire of Love
A dateless lively heat, still to endure,
And grew a seething bath, which yet men prove
Against strange maladies a sovereign cure.
But at my mistress' eye Love's brand new-fired,
The boy for trial needs would touch my breast ;
I, sick withal, the help of bath desired,
And thither hied, a sad distemper'd guest,
  But found no cure : the bath for my help lies
  Where Cupid got new fire—my mistress' eyes.

(II.)

The little Love-god lying once asleep
Laid by his side his heart-inflaming brand,

Whilst many nymphs that vow'd chaste life to keep
Came tripping by ; but in her maiden hand
The fairest votary took up that fire
Which many legions of true hearts had warm'd ;
And so the general of hot desire
Was sleeping by a virgin hand disarm'd.
This brand she quenched in a cool well by,
Which from Love's fire took heat perpetual,
Growing a bath and healthful remedy
For men diseased ; but I, my mistress' thrall,
  Came there for cure, and this by that I prove,
  Love's fire heats water, water cools not love.

XIV.

AS IT FELL UPON A DAY

As it fell upon a day
In the merry month of May,
Sitting in a pleasant shade
Which a grove of myrtles made,
Beasts did leap, and birds did sing,
Trees did grow, and plants did spring ;
Every thing did banish moan,
Save the nightingale alone :

She, poor bird, as all forlorn,
Lean'd her breast up-till a thorn,
And there sung the dolefull'st ditty,
That to hear it was great pity :
'Fie, fie, fie,' now would she cry ;
'Tereu, tereu !' by and by ;
That to hear her so complain,
Scarce I could from tears refrain ;
For her griefs, so lively shown,
Made me think upon mine own.
Ah, thought I, thou mourn'st in vain !
None takes pity on thy pain :
Senseless trees they cannot hear thee ;
Ruthless beasts they will not cheer thee :
King Pandion he is dead ;
All thy friends are lapp'd in lead;
All thy fellow birds do sing,
Careless of thy sorrowing.
Even so, poor bird, like thee,
None alive will pity me.
Whilst as fickle fortune smiled,
Thou and I were both beguiled.
Every one that flatters thee
Is no friend in misery.
Words are easy, like the wind ;
Faithful friends are hard to find :

Every man will be thy friend
Whilst thou hast wherewith to spend ;
But if store of crowns be scant,
No man will supply thy want.
If that one be prodigal,
Bountiful they will him call,
And with such-like flattering,
' Pity but he were a king ; '
If he be addict to vice,
Quickly him they will entice ;
If to women he be bent,
They have at commandment :
But if Fortune once do frown,
Then farewell his great renown ;
They that fawn'd on him before
Use his company no more.
He that is thy friend indeed,
He will help thee in thy need :
If thou sorrow, he will weep ;
If thou wake, he cannot sleep ;
Thus of every grief in heart
He with thee doth bear a part.
These are certain signs to know
Faithful friend from flattering foe.

XV.

IF LOVE MAKE ME FORSWORN.

If love make me forsworn, how shall I swear to love?
O never faith could hold, if not to beauty vow'd:
Though to myself forsworn, to thee I'll constant prove;
Those thoughts, to me like oaks, to thee like osiers bow'd.
Study his bias leaves, and makes his book thine eyes,
Where all those pleasures live that art can comprehend.
If knowledge be the mark, to know thee shall suffice;
Well learned is that tongue that well can thee commend;
All ignorant that soul that sees thee without wonder;
Which is to me some praise, that I thy parts admire:
Thine eye Jove's lightning seems, thy voice his dreadful
    thunder,
Which, not to anger bent, is music and sweet fire.
  Celestial as thou art, O do not love that wrong,
  To sing heaven s praise with such an earthly tongue.

The Passionate Pilgrim, v.

XVI.

A WOMAN.

Fair is my love, but not so fair as fickle ;
Mild as a dove, but neither true nor trusty ;
Brighter than glass, and yet, as glass is, brittle ;
Softer than wax, and yet, as iron, rusty :
    A lily pale, with damask dye to grace her,
    None fairer, nor none falser to deface her.

Her lips to mine how often hath she join'd,
Between each kiss her oaths of true love swearing !
How many tales to please me hath she coin'd,
Dreading my love, the loss thereof still fearing !
    Yet, in the midst of all her pure protestings,
    Her faith, her oaths, her tears, and all were jestings.

She burn'd with love, as straw with fire flameth ;
She burn'd out love, as soon as straw out-burneth ;
She framed the love, and yet she foil'd the framing ;
She bade love last, and yet she fell a-turning.
    Was this a lover, or a lecher whether ?
    Bad in the best, though excellent in neither.

The Passionate Pilgrim, vii.

XVII.

DEATH IN YOUTH.

Sweet rose, fair flower, untimely pluck'd, soon faded,
Pluck'd in the bud, and faded in the spring !
Bright orient pearl, alack, too timely shaded !
Fair creature, kill'd too soon by death's sharp sting !
   Like a green plum that hangs upon a tree,
   And falls, through wind, before the fall should be.

I weep for thee, and yet no cause I have ;
For why thou left'st me nothing in thy will :
And yet thou left'st me more than I did crave ;
For why I craved nothing of thee still :
   O yes, dear friend, I pardon crave for thee,
   Thy discontent thou didst bequeath to me.

The Passionate Pilgrim, x.

XVIII.

YOUTH AND AGE.

Crabbed age and youth cannot live together :
Youth is full of pleasance, age is full of care ;

Youth like summer morn, age like winter weather;
Youth like summer brave, age like winter bare.
Youth is full of sport, age's breath is short;
  Youth is nimble, age is lame ;
Youth is hot and bold, age is weak and cold ;
  Youth is wild, and age is tame.
Age, I do abhor thee ; youth, I do adore thee ;
  O, my love, my love is young !
Age, I do defy thee : O, sweet shepherd, hie thee,
  For methinks thou stay'st too long.

The Passionate Pilgrim, xii.

XIX.

BEAUTY.

BEAUTY is but a vain and doubtful good ;
A shining gloss that fadeth suddenly ;
A flower that dies when first it gins to bud ;
A brittle glass that's broken presently :
    A doubtful good, a gloss, a glass, a flower,
    Lost, faded, broken, dead within an hour.

And as goods lost are seld or never found,
As faded glass no rubbing will refresh,

As flowers dead lie wither'd on the ground,
As broken glass no cement can redress,
So beauty blemish'd once's for ever lost,
In spite of physic, painting, pain and cost.

The Passionate Pilgrim, xiii.

XX.

GOOD NIGHT, GOOD REST.

GOOD night, good rest.   Ah, neither be my share:
She bade good night that kept my rest away;
And daff'd me to a cabin hang'd with care,
To descant on the doubts of my decay.
  'Farewell,' quoth she, 'and come again to-morrow;'
  Farewell, I could not, for I supp'd with sorrow.

Yet at my parting sweetly did she smile,
In scorn or friendship, will I construe whether:
'T may be, she joy'd to jest at my exile,
'T may be, again to make me wander thither:
  'Wander,' a word for shadows like myself,
  As take the pain, but cannot pluck the pelf.

The Passionate Pilgrim, xiv.

XXI.

LOVE LONGING.

Lord, how mine eyes throw gazes to the east !
My heart doth charge the watch ; the morning rise
Doth cite each moving sense from idle rest.
Not daring trust the office of mine eyes,
    While Philomela sits and sings, I sit and mark,
    And wish her lays were tuned like the lark ;

For she doth welcome daylight with her ditty,
And drives away dark dismal-dreaming night :
The night so pack'd, I post unto my pretty ;
Heart hath his hope, and eyes their wished sight ;
    Sorrow changed to solace, solace mixed with sorrow ;
    For why, she sigh'd, and bade me come to-morrow.

Were I with her, the night would post too soon ;
But now are minutes added to the hours ;
To spite me now, each minute seems a moon ;
Yet not for me, shine sun to succour flowers !
    Pack night, peep day ; good day, of night now borrow :
    Short, night, to-night, and length thyself to-morrow.

                The Passionate Pilgrim, xv.

XXII.

THE PHŒNIX AND THE TURTLE.

LET the bird of loudest lay,
On the sole Arabian tree,
Heralds sad and trumpets be,
To whose sounds chaste wings obey.

But thou shrieking harbinger,
Foul precurrer of the fiend,
Augur of the fever's end,
To this troop come thou not near.

From this session interdict
Every fowl of tyrant wing,
Save the eagle, feather'd king :
Keep the obsequy so strict.

Let the priest in surplice white,
That defunctive music can,
Be the death-divining swan,
Lest the requiem lack his right.

And thou treble-dated crow,
That thy sable gender makest

With the breath thou givest and takest,
'Mongst our mourners shall thou go.

Here the anthem doth commence:
Love and constancy is dead;
Phœnix and the turtle fled
In a mutual flame from hence.

So they loved, as love in twain
Had the essence but in one;
Two distincts, division none;
Number there in love was slain.

Hearts remote, yet not asunder;
Distance, and no space was seen
'Twixt the turtle and his queen:
But in them it were a wonder.

So between them love did shine,
That the turtle saw his right
Flaming in the phœnix' sight;
Either was the other's mine.

Property was thus appalled,
That the self was not the same;
Single nature's double name
Neither two nor one was called.

Reason, in itself confounded,
Saw division grow together,
To themselves yet either neither,
Simply were so well compounded,

That it cried, How true a twain
Seemeth this concordant one !
Love hath reason, reason none,
If what parts can so remain.

Whereupon it made this threne
To the phœnix and the dove,
Co-supremes and stars of love,
As chorus to their tragic scene.

THRENOS.

Beauty, truth, and rarity,
Grace in all simplicity,
Here enclosed in cinders lie.

Death is now the phœnix' nest ;
And the turtle's loyal breast
To eternity doth rest,

Leaving no posterity :
'Twas not their infirmity,
It was married chastity.

Truth may seem, but cannot be ;
Beauty brag, but 'tis not she ;
Truth and beauty buried be.

To this urn let those repair
That are either true or fair ;
For these dead birds sigh a prayer,

XXIII.

KNOWLEDGE.

Crowns have their compass, length of days their date,
Triumphs their tomb, Felicity her fate :
Of naught but earth can Earth make us partaker,
But knowledge makes a king most like his Maker.

XXIV.

LAST WORDS.

He that no more must say is listen'd more
  Than they whom youth and ease have taught to gloze :
More are men's ends mark'd than their lives before :
  The setting sun, and music at the close,
As the last taste of sweets, is sweetest last,
Writ in remembrance more than things long past.

NOTES TO THE SONNETS.

No. i.—The *motif* of this and others of the succeeding sonnets is treated in like manner in *Venus and Adonis*. (Lines 162-174.)

Line 10. 'Only herald:" the word 'only' here has not the significance which it now commonly bears. 'Matchless,' 'incomparable,' 'choicest,' may be regarded as synonymus. As already noted in the preface, the words in the original prefatory announcement of the Sonnets—'onlie begetter'—do not mean 'the solitary procurer,' but, probably, the 'Incomparable Inspirer.'

No. iii.—Lines 9, 10. Compare with lines 1758-9, in *Lucrece*,

> 'Poor broken glass, I often did behold
> In thy sweet semblance my old age new-born.'

Lines 13, 14, *i.e.*—If you *will* live without perpetuating your race, then, dying single, your beauty (the likeness of your beauty) must die also.

No. v.—Line 1. *Hours.* Here this word is a dissyllable.

Lines 9, 10. Allusive to perfumes in glass or crystal flagons, the distillation of the sweetest flowers of summer. (See, for further reference, the opening lines of the ensuing sonnet—also, Sonnet liv., lines 11, 12):—

> ' Sweet roses do not (die),
> Of their sweet deaths are sweetest odours made.'

Line 14. *Leese*—leave.

No. vii.—Line 5. 'Steep-up heavenly hill.' It has been suggested that the reading should be 'steep up-heavenly hill.' Undoubtedly there is more apparent redundancy in 'steep-up' than in 'up-heavenly'; but as for another objection that has been put forward—that there is nothing in the text to justify reference to a 'heavenly' hill—there is no basis, the meaning being quite clear, the 'heavenly hill' being of course the sky, up which the 'burning head' of the sun mounts as the new day grows.

Moreover, compare with the 4th line of the 9th division of *The Passionate Pilgrim*, where 'steep-up' again occurs.

No. viii.—Line 14.   A reference to the saying that 'one is no number,' a statement more clearly made in Sonnet cxxxvi., line 8,

'Among a number one is reckoned none.

No. ix.—Line 4. 'Makeless.' An early English word (Ang: Sax :) signifying companionless. *Mak* or *maca*, a companion. Used at least once by Chaucer. Thus, also, the Earl of Surrey, in his Sonnet on Spring—

'*The Turtle to her make hath told her tale.*

No. xi,—Line 11.   Should not this line run—

'*Thou*, whom she best endow'd,' etc.

No. xiii.—Line 6. 'Determination in legal language means end.' (Malone.)

No. xiv.—Line 8. 'By oft predict'—*i.e.*, by prediction often made. It is quite possible that Sewell's reading (Ed. 2.) 'By ought predict' is the right one. 'By any prediction that I in heaven find' is certainly as likely as 'By frequent predictions'; while 'by ought predict' is clearer than 'by oft predict.' On the other hand, compare with this the use of 'suspect' for 'suspicion,' in *Venus and Adonis* (line 1010)—

'*Her rash suspect she doth extenuate.*

Lines 11, 12, 14. I here follow Professor Dowden's precedent in the addition of inverted commas : the gain in clearness is distinct.

No. xv. *Suggestion.* Might not the last line have originally run—

'As he takes from you, I engraft anew.'

The three 'you's' so close together, and the terminal 'you now'—a combination hardly likely to please Shakespeare's keen ear—would thus be modified, while the sense would be as clear or even clearer. The printing of ' you now' for 'anew' would have been a slip of earliest occurrence.

No. xvi.—Line 9. I quote from Professor Dowden :—

Lines of Life—i.e., ' children.' The unusual expression is selected because it suits the imagery of the sonnet, lines applying to (1) Lineage, (2) delineation with a pencil, a portrait, (3) lines of verse as in xviii, 12. Lines of life are living lines, living poems and pictures, children.'

No. xvii.—Line 12. Keats selected this line as a motto for *Endymion.* Professor Dowden says that ' stretched metre ' is ' overstrained poetry ' : it was probably not, however, in this sense that Keats understood the phrase, but as referring to the somewhat loose metrical construction of early versification.

No. xxi.—Line 8. *Rondure* or *roundure* means a circle. The word occurs several times in the writings of Elizabethan poets, and Shakespeare himself has used it elsewhere (*vide King John*, Act ii. Sc. 1 :—'The roundure of your old-faced walls.') While the line as it stands certainly does not call imperatively for any alteration, there can be no doubt but that Staunton's suggestion of ' vault ' in place of ' air ' would, if given effect to, add much to the music of the octave—the unpleasant assurance of the terminal ' rare ' (line 7), and ' air ' so early in the next line being very noticeable in the accepted text.

Line 12 'As those gold candles fix'd in heaven's air.' Calling the stars 'those gold candles' was a thoroughly Elizabethan conceit, but that it was more than a mere passing fancy with Shakespeare is manifest from the fact that he was not content with its single adoption : thus we have

' These blessed candles of the night.'

Merchant of Venice, Act v. line 220.

'Their candles are all out.'

Macbeth, Act ii. Sc. 1.,

and those beautiful lines in Romeo's famous speech in the balcony overlooking Capulet's orchard—

'Night's candles are burnt out, and jocund day
Stands tiptoe on the misty mountain-tops.'

Romeo and Juliet, Act iii. Sc. v.

Possibly the idea of ' candles ' or ' lamps ' was first suggested to Shakespeare by lines in the plays of his great forerunner, Christopher Marlowe—*e.g.*, 'And the ceaseless

lamps That gently look'd upon this loathsome earth,' etc.—
Tamburlaine, Act ii. Sc. 4 ; and again, ' that shine as bright as
all the lamps that beautify the sky.'—*Tamburlaine*, Act v.
Sc. 3. Compare, also, Spenser's ' At last fair Hesperus . . .
Had spent his lamp.'

No. xxiv—Lines 1, 2.

Stell'd, fixed ; *table*, tablet (*tabula*), that which in art-
phraseology is called a panel, or polished wooden slab on
which a picture is painted.

No. xxviii—Line 12. *Twire* or *tweere* : old English for ' peep.'

Line 14. Professor Dowden adheres to the Quarto, and
prints—

' And night doth nightly made grief's *length* seem stronger.'

No. xxix.—Line 12. Compare with this line the first of the
beautiful lark-song from *Cymbeline*, No. xxxvii. among the
Songs.

No. xxxi.—Lines 13, 14. That is—The very image of each
departed friend whom I loved, I now view in thee—and thou,
having every charm of theirs added to thine own, hast
absolutely my sole and undivided devotion.

No. xxxii.—It is generally agreed that this sonnet reads as
though it were an envoy, and taking it as such, I have drawn
a line beneath it.

No. xxxiii.—A new series undoubtedly begins here, a series
dealing with a wrong done to Shakespeare by his friend.

No. xxxv —Line 8. *i.e.*, finding excuses even to a further
length than his friend could possibly sin.

No. xxxviii.—Line 14. The word ' pain ' I take here not to
mean ' suffering ' or ' punishment ' (see Note to Sonnet 141),
but ' *labour*.'

No. xxxix.—Line 12. The brackets are not in the accepted text,
but they are an aid to clearness.

Lines 13, 14. In other words, Shakespeare emphasises the
fact that love, deprived of the physical aspect of its object, can
yet delight in the mental likeness treasured up of the absent
one. Compare—

' Or heart in love with sighs himself doth smother,
With my love's picture then my eye doth feast
And to the painted banquet bids my heart.'
No. xlvii. Lines 4-6.

No. xliii.—Line 13. I have adopted Malone's conjectural reading (vol. xx., p. 267), in place of the stereotyped ' All days are nights to see till I see thee.'

No. l.—The placing in italics of lines 4 and 14 seems to me an improvement.

No. li.—Line 11 and lines 13, 14. In both instances I have followed Professor Dowden: in the first, by discarding this generally accepted version—

> ' Shall neigh—no dull flesh—in his fiery race,'

(*i.e.*, that in Desire's impetuous pursuit there is nothing of impulse that is not impassioned.) In the second place, by adding inverted commas to the concluding couplet, it being spoken by ' Love.'

No. liii.—Lines 1-4. Compare with ' He sees himself in all he sees,' and other corresponding lines in *In Memoriam.*

Line 9. *Foison :* abundance—*i.e.*, as spring is but a reflex of the beauty of his friend, so the natural plenty of autumn is as the latter's ' bounty ' of noble qualities.

No. liv.—Line 4. Comparison between this and a corresponding line in Sonnet v. has already been suggested.

Line 5. *Canker-blooms :* wild roses.

No. lvi.—Line 6. Shakespeare uses *wink* in the sense of ' sleep, or ' droop with sleep,' or ' drowsy,' on two or three occasions. *E.g.*, in ' winking mary-buds,' in the lark-song in *Cymbeline.*

Line 8. *Dulness :* probably signifying slumber. Compare *The Tempest*, Act i. Sc. 2., where Prospero, referring to Miranda's sleep, exclaims, '' Tis a good dulness.'

Line 13.—*Else*, etc., is the generally accepted reading. The Quarto has *as.* Professor Dowden prints *or.* There seems no reason for departure from the use of ' else.'

No. lvii.—Line 13. Though the word ' will ' in the penultimate line is printed in the Quarto with a capital ' W,' it does not necessarily follow that any extra significance is therein embodied : there are several other words in the Quarto which have capital initials—*e.g.*, *Alien, Autumn, Satire*, etc.—but which convey no double meaning. At the same time it is quite likely that a similar play on words is intended as occurs in Sonnets cxxxv. and cxxxvi. ; and in this sense the present Editor accepts the Quarto reading. Those who, notwithstanding the possibility of ' will ' having the same double significance in Sonnets lvii. and cxxxvi. (along with the fact of the Quarto capital-initial) may not feel inclined to accept this version, will agree with the lines as they appear in the Globe Edition, in Professor Dowden's, and elsewhere :—

> 'So true a fool is love that in your will,
>   Though you do anything he thinks no ill,'

i.e., 'So true a fool is love (the love I have for you) that, whatever act you may commit, he will discover no evil in your intention.'

No. lviii.—Line 1.   I have added brackets to the subsidiary phrase.

No. lix.—Lines 1, 2.

> 'If there be nothing new, but that which is,
>   Hath been before,' etc

Compare with this the 3rd stanza in Rossetti's *Sudden Light.*

> 'Has this been thus before?
>   And shall not thus Time's eddying flight
>   Still with our lives our love restore
>   In Death's despite,
> And day and night yield one delight once more ?'

Line 11.   The Cambridge editors read

> ' *Whether we are mended, or whether better they,*'

a version at once unpleasant to the ear and dissentient from the text.   In the Quarto the line runs ' Whether we are mended, or where better they '—the ' where ' here being ' whether ' pronounced as a monosyllable (a variation of not infrequent occurrence in the Elizabethan writers).   Dyce reads ' Whether we're mended, or whêr better they,' but the Editor thinks it better to follow Dowden's example and keep to the Quarto, with the exception of spelling ' whe'r ' for ' where '

No. lx.—Line 13.   *Times in Hope :* times to come, future times.

No. lxiv.   Of this and the two succeeding sonnets Mr. Palgrave well says ' these three sonnets form one poem of marvellous power, insight, and beauty.'

Lines 9-14. Compare herewith the following lines by Rossetti, the most Shakespearian of all subsequent sonneteers :—

> 'O love, my love! if I no more should see
> Thyself, nor on the earth the shadow of thee,
>   Nor image of thine eyes in any spring,—

How then should sound upon Life's darkening slope
The ground-whirl of the perished leaves of Hope,
    The wind of Death's imperishable wing?'
            The House of Life. No. iv. ' Lovesight.'

' Not I myself know all my love for thee :
    How should I reach so far, who cannot weigh
    To-morrow's dower by gage of yesterday?
Shall birth and death, and all dark names that be
As doors and windows bared to some loud sea,
    Lash deaf mine ears and blind my face with spray ;
    And shall my sense pierce love,—the last relay
And ultimate outpost of eternity?'
            The House of Life. No. xxxiv. 'The Dark Glass.'

No. lxv.—Line 10.   The generally accepted reading is—

' Shall Time's best jewel from Time's chest lie hid.'

'Chest' was several times used by Shakespeare in the sense
of casket, treasure-place : but I agree with Theobald in
preferring ' quest ' as the proper reading.   Malone once held
this view, but afterwards believed 'chest' to be correct.
(*Vide*, for argument and illustration, *Malone*, vol. xx.
pp. 283-4.)

But could 'a jewel lie hid' *from* a chest?   It 'lies hid'
from the eager quest of destroying Time, whose 'swift
foot' no 'strong hand' can hold back, whose 'spoliation
of beauty' no one 'can forbid.'

No. lxvii.—Line 4.   *Lace*, embellish.   Line 6.—*Seeming*,
generally printed *seeing*.

No. lxviii.—Line 3.   *Fair*, beauty.

No. lxxiv.—Line 11. Does this refer to assassination, or to
the dissector's knife?

No. lxxvi. ' Is this an apology for Shakespeare's own sonnets
—of which his friend begins to weary—in contrast with the
verses of the rival poet, spoken of in lxxviii-lxxx?'
            —*Professor Dowden.*

Line 6—*i.e.*, In a known, a recognisable style.

No. lxxvii. It has been surmised (Steevens, Malone, etc.) that
this sonnet accompanied a present of a book of blank
leaves, to be used as a diary by his friend, (Lines 9, 10).

No. lxxx.—Line 2. *A 'better spirit:* now understood to be Chapman. (*Vide* different commentators, especially Minto.)

'Was it the proud full sail of his great verse,'
(No. lxxxvi. Line 1.)

could only be considered specially applicable to two men other than Shakespeare himself, Marlowe and Chapman.

No. lxxxiv.—Line 11. *Fame his wit '—i.e.,* make famous his brilliant intellectual powers.

Line 14. Palgrave prints 'fond of,' but that Shakespeare wrote 'fond on ' is fairly manifest from similar usage in *Midsummer Night's Dream.* Act ii. Sc. 1.

'More fond on her than she upon his love.'

No. lxxxvii.—Line 8, *patent:* privilege ; line, 11, *misprision:* mistake.

No. xc.—Line 1. Mr. Hall Caine (*Sonnets of Three Centuries —Notes*) suggests—

'Then hate me, an' thou wilt, if ever, now.'

Doubtless 'an' thou wilt' reads better than 'when,' etc., though the 'when ' certainly presents no ' baffling difficulty': his version, however, is no improvement in punctuation, the comma at 'wilt' in place of the semi-colon being a distinct mistake.

No. xci. Sonnets xci , cx., cxi., and cxii. have a counterpart in *Hamlet,* Act iii. Sc. 2 :—

' When in disgrace with fortune and men's eyes,
I all alone beweep my outcast state,' etc.

As M. Taine (p. 167, Vol. I, *Hist. Lit.*) points out, these 'paroles d'Hamlet sont moins bien placées dans la bouche d'un prince que dans celle de l' auteur.'

No. xcii.—Line 14. This line occurs in *King Edward III.,* Act. ii. Sc. 1. The probability is that the line in the sonnet was reminiscent. *Weeds,* the rhyme word to *deeds,* reca'' ed the line in the play, otherwise also applicable : and this whether the play was by Shakespeare or not.

No. xcvi.—Lines 13-14. Identical with the couplet at the close of xxxvi.

No. xcviii. To the lines 3, 4 of this sonnet, to which he applies the poetic heading *The Garden of Love,* Mr. Palgrave appends the note :—' *Heavy Saturn:* the gloomy side of nature: or, the saturnine spirit in life.'

Line 11.—*i.e.*, The rose and lily were sweet, they were figures—emblems—of delight, only in so far as they suggested Shakespeare's beloved friend, 'pattern of all' lovely things.

No. xcix.—This sonnet has fifteen lines.
I print 'froward violet' instead of 'forward violet.'
Line 14.—*i.e.*, 'but *scent* or colour,' as in line 7 of cxxv :—

'*For compound sweet foregoing simple savour.*'

No. c.—This Sonnet may be, as Professor Dowden suggests, the commencement of a new series after a prolonged period of silence on account of preoccupation with dramatic production. But it may also afford a clue towards dating this section of the Sequence, for it may contain a reference to the 'Dark Woman' series: here S. may have noted his turning away from the deceitful love of an evil woman to the steadfast affection and regard of a true friend :—

'Sing, instead of wasting thy poetic enthusiasm on some worthless song—misusing thy power in casting a glamour over base subjects—

'Sing to the ear that dost thy lays esteem,
And gives thy pen both skill and argument.'

No. civ.—Lines 9, 10. *i.e.*, Steal from the figure on the dial.

No. cix.—This sonnet reads like a reply to an accusation of forgetfulness, and, moreover, like one sent to the Beloved Friend during or after the season of his (Shakespeare's) love for the Dark Woman.

No. cx.—Lines 1-3. An allusion to the time when he was himself a strolling player.
Line 13. May not the 'my heaven' here be an allusion to his mistress?

No. cxi.—Line 10. *Eisel:* vinegar. The allusion is to the supposed potency of vinegar against infection.

No. cxiii.—Line 14. *i.e.*, The transmuting power of love acts so potently mentally, in his case, that it makes even his eye an unfaithful recorder of visible familiar objects—each 'mountain or sea,' 'crow or dove,' seeming no longer itself, but 'shaping' itself to the 'feature' of his friend.

No. cxix.—Line 2. *Limbecks:* alembics.

No. **cxx.**   It is possible that this sonnet is, as regarded by Dr. Burgersdijk, a defence of the Stage against Puritans (*Dowden*) —bnt it may merely refer to the jealous detractors whom Shakespeare's growing reputation stung into spiteful insinuations and distorted half truths.

Line 11.   *Level :* crooked.   As Steevens pointed out, a term used only by masons and joiners.

No. **cxxii.**   This sonnet reads as if S.'s friend had upbraided him for having parted with the ' tables '—manuscript-book—(perhaps a diary ; perhaps a *confessio amantis* corresponding to S.'s sonnets ; more likely, mere jottings concerning the writer's opinions on matters of taste and current events).   Shakespeare rebuts the accusation, adding (lines 13, 14) that he needs no object to keep his love always in mental vision, that keeping such an object would imply probable or possible forgetfulness.

No. **cxxiv.**—Line 1.   *i.e.,* ' The child of high estate.'

Line 13.   ' *To this I witness call the fools of time.*'   I am inclined to think that this means ' As witnesses to the fact that my love is ' builded far from accident, I summon those very detractors, those fools of a season, who, though they have lived to my harm, will thus ultimately still further cement our love.'

Mr. Palgrave suggests ' the plotters and political martyrs of the age,' but the relevancy, save in connection with ' state ' (line 1) is not very manifest.

No. **cxxvi.**   This is not a sonnet, but a short poem of six rhymed couplets.   It is the Envoy to the preceding Sequence.   The meaning of the last eight lines is ' That nature only keeps you in your flawless beauty for her own delight   Beware of her, for while she may keep you yet awhile in all delight of life, she will, soon or late, have to give you up—choicest of her treasured things though you be—to Time.   To this unappeasable creditor she must pay her debt at last.'

No. **cxxvii.**   The series that now commences might fittingly have for heading a line from *Love's Labour's Lost,* Act iv. Sc. 3,

' *And therefore is she born to make black fair,*

and be preceded by those scathing lines printed in this volume, among the poems, under the title ' A Woman.'

No. **cxxviii.**—Line 5.   *Envy* is here pronounced envý.   *Jacks* is a term for the keys of the virginal.

No. cxxix. Compare with the lines from *Venus and Adonis*, quoted here among the Poems under the title '*Love.*'

No. cxxx. It has been supposed by some commentators that this sonnet was written with ironical reference to the conventional praises of beauty then so much in vogue. As Professor Minto says, it reads like a defiant assertion of veracity even in poetic language. On the other hand, the sonnet is so manifestly part and portion of the series in which it was embedded that, granted the genuineness of the Dark Woman Theory, there can be no doubt of its applicability to the woman whom Shakespeare loved so strongly, against his better judgment.

No. cxxxii.—Lines 7-9. Compare with these beautiful lines Marlowe's famous simile applied to Helen of Troy :—

> ' O, thou art fairer than the evening air
>   Clad in the beauty of a thousand stars.'

>> *Doctor Faustus.* Act v. Sc. 3.

No. cxxxiii. Compare this sonnet with xlii. This must have been written at the time of his beloved's unfaithfulness, and No. xlii. reminiscently. The same strain of argument runs through both.

No. cxxxv. As in lvii., and also in cxxxvi., there is a play upon '*will.*' '*Will*' in the first line probably signifies '*desire,*' '*wish.*'

'*Will*' at the beginning of the second line, the Christian name of Shakespeare's friend and successful rival (*W. H.?* William Herbert, Earl of Pembroke? There can be no doubt, when it is remembered that Mrs. Fitton, the too fascinating maid-of-honour who gained such superfluity of devotion, had an illegitimate child by William, Earl of Pembroke, *Shakespeare's* Earl).

'*Will*' at the end of the second line, Shakespeare himself : (evident from the immediate continuity of the succeeding half dozen words.)

It is quite possible that, as Professor Dowden suggests, there may be a dual meaning in the first '*will,*'—*viz.*, that it may also contain a reference to the lady's husband. This, of course, is pure conjecture, for the Christian name of both Mrs. Fitton's husbands—Captain Lougher and Captain Polwhele—are unknown.

Line 13. I follow Professor Dowden in the reading of this line. The line has hitherto always stood 'Let no unkind, no fair beseechers kill.'   Many speculations have been made as to its real meaning; it has been surmised that *unkind* is a substantive, meaning the Unkind one (the unyielding mistress], in the same way that 'fair' was often used.   The significance of the line, however, remains as occult as before.   Mr. W. M. Rossetti made a clever guess when he proposed the substitution of 'skill' for *kill*, 'skill' bearing its old significance, *avail* or *profit:*—thus, 'Let no unkind, no fair beseechers, avail to dissuade you from this argument.'   But there is hardly enough evidence to make it seem probable that S. wrote 'skill' instead of 'kill' with the meaning referred to by Mr. Rossetti.   The present editor takes the line to mean— 'Let no unkind rejection of them kill [do away with, negative] such fair arguments (beseechers)', and he has consequently adopted the reading suggested by Professor Dowden, who, however, understands it, 'Let no unkind refusal kill fair beseechers.'   Line 9.   The terminals of lines 3 and 9 are identical. As there is no other variation on 'will' throughout the terminals, it has frequently occurred to me that the last word of the penultimate line may also have been 'still'—the line in this case could still bear the same meaning as that accepted above: for 'still,' as a verb, could signify subdue, put away from, negative.

No. cxxxvi.—Line 10.   In most editions printed *stores* or *stores*': but store's, as pointed out by Schmidt, Dowden, etc., is manifestly correct.

Sonnet entitled ' *Vows.*'   I have had no scruple in inserting in the stereotyped sequence this sonnet from *The Passionate Pilgrim* (the same that appears with variations in *Love's Labour's Lost*, Act iv. Sc. 3)—though of course without causing any break in the universally-accepted numeration.   In the first place, two other sonnets from *The Passionate Pilgrim* (the two immediately preceding this sonnet on Vows—the three respectively forming Divisions i., ii., and iii. of *The Passionate Pilgrim*) appear in the regular sequence—namely, Nos. cxxxviii. and cxliv.

As there are differences in the two versions, and as that printed in the text corresponds with the version in the play, the older (?) from *The Passionate Pilgrim* is here added:—

(III.)

Did not the heavenly rhetoric of thine eye,
'Gainst whom the world could not hold argument,
Persuade my heart to this false perjury?
Vows for thee broke deserve not punishment,

A woman I forswore ; but I will prove,
Thou being a goddess, I forswore not thee :
My vow was earthly, thou a heavenly love ;
Thy grace being gain'd cures all disgrace in me,
My vow was breath, and breath a vapour is ;
Then, thou fair sun, that on this earth doth shine,
Exhale this vapour vow ; in thee it is :
If broken, then it is no fault of mine.
 If by me broke, what fool is not so wise
 To break an oath, to win a paradise ?

In the next place, it seems to me to fit in here with peculiar applicability. It is the last time that S. hints there is anything more in his love than thraldom to a strong and subtle passion ; while there is also a suggestion of the feebleness of spiritual resolution struggling against the 'power of the flesh,' of vows being as vapour, with the half-passionate. half-cynical conclusion—

 " If by me broke, what fool is not so wise
  To break an oath, to win a paradise ? "

To the possible objection that S. would never have addressed the lady of Sonnet cxxx. as "thou fair sun," etc. (10th line), there could be opposed the line in Sonnet cxlvii.—

 " For I have sworn thee fair and thought thee bright."

(See also Sonnet clii. lines 13-14.)

No. cxxxvii.—Lines 9, 10. Mr. Halliwell explains the allusion in the words 'several' and 'common' by stating that enclosed fields were of two descriptions, those belonging to the inhabitants collectively getting the name of commons, those (also portions of enclosed commons, fenced in, and which had been allotted to owners of freeholds, cottages, etc) belonging to individuals were called 'severals.' Thus (as pointed out by Professor Dowden) in *Love's Labour's Lost* (Act ii. sc. 1)—

 ' *My lips are no* COMMON *though* SEVERAL *they be.*

No. cxxxviii. This sonnet is an amended version of the first of those that appear in *The Passionate Pilgrim.* The latter, the original, I append here :—

(LOVE'S HABIT.

I.

When my love swears that she is made of truth,
I do believe her, though I know she lies,

c-18-c

That she might think me some untutor'd youth,
Unskilful in the world's false forgeries.
Thus vainly thinking that she thinks me young,
Although I know my years be past the best,
I smiling credit her false-speaking tongue,
Outfacing faults in love with love's ill rest.
But wherefore says my love that she is young?
And wherefore say not I that I am old?
O, love's best habit is a soothing tongue,
And age, in love, loves not to have years told.
  Therefore, I'll lie with love, and love with me,
  Since that our faults in love thus smother'd be.

Compare, again, with the lines among the Poems, 'A Woman.'

'Love in Tears' (between cxxxix. and cxl.): as stated in the Preface, this sonnet comes from *Love's Labour's Lost* (Act iv. Sc. 3, ll. 28-40)   I believe this is the first time these lines have been printed as a sonnet, or that they have been so dissociated from the text as to be considered a sonnet at all.   Of course, as heretofore said, my insertion of '*Love in Tears*' in the place it occupies in this edition is purely conjectural.

No. cxli.—Line 14, *last word*.   'Pain in its old etymological sense of punishment.'   W. S. Walker, *Crit. Exam. of the Text of Shakespeare.*

No. cxliii.—Line 13.   Here, again, there is a play upon the word 'will.'   The obvious reading is that Shakespeare will be content if, having once gained the love of his friend and rival, and having gratified her *will* in her acquisition, she will but turn back to his loyal devotion.

No. cxliv.   The second of the three sonnets at the beginning of *The Passionate Pilgrim*.   The variations are not so important as in the case of No. cxxxviii.   They are as follows :—Line 2, '*That like*'; line 3, '*my better angel*'; line 4, '*my* worser spirit'; line 8, '*fair* pride'; line 11, '*for* being both *to* me'; line 13, '*the truth I shall not know*.'   The Quarto has also (*line* 6), 'from my *sight*,' a manifest misprint.

No student of our later sonnet-literature need be reminded of the renascence of Shakespeare's influence in recent years.   Of course the most marked instance is that of the sonnet-work of Rossetti, where the weightiness of diction (combined with "fundamental brain-work") is beyond that of any other maker of 'deep-brain'd sonnettes' subsequent to the great dramatist himself.   As a good example of this Shake-

spearian influence, and, morever, in what may be called con-
sanguineous relation to this 144th Sonnet, I may quote the
following exceedingly fine sonnet by Mr. John Addington
Symonds :—

> Spirit of light and darkness! I no less
>   Twy-natured, but of more terraqueous mould,
>   In whom conflicting powers proportion hold
> With poise exact, before thy proud excess
> Of beauty perfect and pure lawlessness
>   Quail self-confounded; neither nobly bold
>   To dare for thee damnation, nor so cold
>   As to endure unscathed thy fiery stress.
> Both of thine angels wound me; and so tame
>   Is this mixt essence of my earthlier mind,
>   That seeking joy of sense, I light on shame;
> Flying from shame, desire's loath'd dungeon find;
>   Attack, retreat; clasp and unclasp; and win
>   Neither the wage of virtue nor of sin.
>
> *Vagabunduli Libellus.* No. liv., p. 64.

No. cxlv.   This is not a sonnet-proper at all, consisting as it
does of octosyllabic instead of decasyllabic lines. It is even
doubtful if it is really by Shakespeare. In any case it here
seems out of place, and reads but poorly indeed in conjunction
with such noble sonnets as those immediately preceding and
following. Possibly it had been mistakingly inserted by
'T. T.' in place of 'Vows' (see intermediary sonnet, between
cxxxvi. and cxxxvii).

No. cxlvi.—Line 2.   Generally this line is printed with asterisks
for the two missing words at the commencement. In the
Quarto there is a manifest printer's error, a repetition of the
last two words of the first line.

   Of all the suggested substitutions—'Fool'd by' (Malone,
Dyce, Palgrave, Caine, etc.); 'Starv'd by the' (Steevens);
'Hemmed with these' (Furnivall); ' *My sinful earth these rebel
powers array*' (Gerald Massey); 'My sins these' (Bullock);
'Foil'd by' (F. T. Palgrave); 'Slave of these' (Cartwright);
'Press'd by' (Dowden); 'Leagu'd with these' (A. E. Brae,
Dr. Ingleby); 'Thrall to these' (Anon.)—it seems to me,
and this is a point each one must settle for himself, for it is
a matter of opinion at best, that perhaps the anonymous
suggestion,'Thrall to these rebel powers,' is the most effective.
Elsewhere S. uses the word 'thrall' somewhat similarly
(' thrall to living death and pain perpetual ').

The word *array* — generally accepted in the sense of
'raimenting'—must surely here bear its old significance,
afflict. The use of *rebel* is itself sufficient to demonstrate that
'array' is not used in the sense of putting on raiment, 'cloth-
ing in flesh': there would be no applicability in 'rebel,' or
'rebellious,' here. 'Rebel powers' plainly signifies antag-
onistic powers, the powers of evil rebellious against the
divine power of the Supreme Good.

I venture to suggest '*Sport of these* rebel powers,' etc.—
because of the strain of part scornful part bitter feeling in
which Shakespeare addresses his soul, the mere sport of the
potent agencies that environ its material investiture and
continuously afflict it : and because the reading seems to me
characteristic.

No. clii.   Here ends the series of sonnets addressed to a
woman.

Nos cliii. and cliv.   The two sonnets, Nos. cliii. and clvi.,
hitherto made practically part and portion of the 'Sonnets,'
probably belong to a much earlier period of Shakespeare's
literary life : in any case they have no distinct connection with
those preceding.   Moreover, each is a different version of the
same *motif.*   They will be found among the Poems under the
title, "Love's Fire."

ADDENDUM.

If the following sonnet be by Shakespeare, as it is considered
by Professor Minto—to whom the merit of its identification as
such (if the fact of its authorship be admitted) is mainly due—it
represents his earliest known composition.   All interested in
the subject must consult Professor Minto's clever piece of
'special pleading' (Appendix *B   Characteristics of English
Poets.   2nd Edition*)—indeed it is necessary to do so before
coming to any judgment.   (See also pp. 218-251 on this subject, in D. M. Main's *Treasury of English Sonnets.*)

John Florio was an eminent teacher of Italian, and was held
in high esteem both by the Court and by men of letters, as is
manifest from the fact of Ben Jonson's having presented to
him a copy of *The Fox* with an inscription setting forth his
friendship and love.   Florio's 'First Fruits' and 'Second
Fruits' were compilations of wise sayings and extracts from

Italian authors of note, and were undoubtedly widely read. The 'Second Fruits' appeared in 1591, and it is to this work which 'Phaeton's' sonnet is prefixed. It is worthy of note also that Florio himself mentions his being then under the patronage of the Earl of Southampton, the same nobleman to whom Shakespeare somewhat later dedicated his *Venus and Adonis* and *Rape of Lucrece*.

PHAETON TO HIS FRIEND FLORIO.

Sweete friend, whose name agrees with thy increase,
   How fit a rivall art thou of the Spring!
   For when each branche hath left his flourishing,
And green-lock'd Summer's shadie pleasures cease,
She makes the Winter's storms repose in peace
   And spends her franchise on each living thing:
   The daisies sprout, the little birds doo sing;
Hearbes, gummes, and plants do vaunt of their release.
So when that all our English witts lay dead
   (Except the Laurell that is ever-greene),
Thou with thy Fruits our barrenness o'erspread
   And set thy flowerie pleasance to be seene.
Such fruits, such flow'rets of moralitie,
Were ne'er before brought out of Italy.

NOTE TO THE SONGS AND POEMS.

Of the delightful and very often exquisite songs scattered throughout Shakespeare's Plays I have no space here to speak in detail. Some are of altogether exceptional beauty, and these seem to be as it were the condensed subtlest aroma of the plays in which they are to be found—as Ophelia's pathetic snatches of weird melody, or as that thrilling song in *Measure for Measure*, where in the Moated Grange at St. Luke's the boy sings before Mariana.

All the songs and snatches of song that could well be excerpted are here to be found; and I trust that my titles, and general presentment of them, may be found satisfactory.

In the section of the *Poems* it will be noted that neither *Venus and Adonis* nor the *Rape of Lucrece* are given in full. In the first place, there was not room for them in complete form; in the second, they are in many portions hardly suited for 'mixed readers' in these days. What seemed to me specially fine therein, and suitable for presentation in this volume, I have excerpted and given under what occurred to me as applicable titles. There can be no doubt that many, to whom these beautiful poems would otherwise remain unread, or at anyrate unenjoyed, will now be able to make acquaintance with some of the finest utterances of the young poet who was in good time to develop into the greatest dramatist the world has seen. For the hint as to 'Stratford Pictures' I am indebted to a note by Mr. Furnival in the *Leopold Shake-speare*: this arrangement is interesting as helping to show the young writer's intimate acquaintance with nature as manifested in the Avonside of his youth. The fine poem, *A Lover's Complaint*, is, however, given intact.

What poetic beauty, what wisdom, what nobility of sentiment and felicity of diction, in these productions of a man still youthful in years! The more we study Shakespeare the more we comprehend the universality of his genius, the more we recognise how truly he is a giant among all men who have ever committed their intellectual riches into the keeping of their fellows.

The lines entitled 'Knowledge' (*Poems*, xxiii.) are given by Mr. R. Grant White at the end of the first volume of his edition of the Life and Works of Shakespeare (*Boston, U.S.A.*) They were first produced in the *Life* by the late Mr. J. P. Collier, who printed them "from a coeval manuscript" containing a short piece by Dekker as well as fragments by many other contemporary dramatists and poets. They may or may not be Shakespeare's, but we can well believe him to have been their author.

'Last Words' (*Poems*, xxiv.) are six lines forming the sestet of a sonnet, and are to be found in *Richard II.*, Act ii. Sc. 1, lines 9-14. They make, indeed, a fitting "music at the close."